About the author

Jenna is a journalism graduate, sci-fi lover, amateur musician and full-time dog enthusiast. She has lived across Canada and attributes the inspiration for her stories to its varying cultures and breathtaking landscapes. Jenna currently calls Calgary, Alberta, home, where she lives with her husband and malamute lapdogs.

LEGENDS OF VARTHIA

Jenna Ephgrave

LEGENDS OF VARTHIA

Vanguard Press

A CIP catalogue record for this title is
available from the British Library.

ISBN 978 1 78465 799 4

*Vanguard Press is an imprint of
Pegasus Elliot MacKenzie Publishers Ltd.*
www.pegasuspublishers.com

First Published in 2020

**Vanguard Press
Sheraton House Castle Park
Cambridge England**

Printed & Bound in Great Britain

Dedication

For my husband who brings out my favourite version
of myself. LYSB

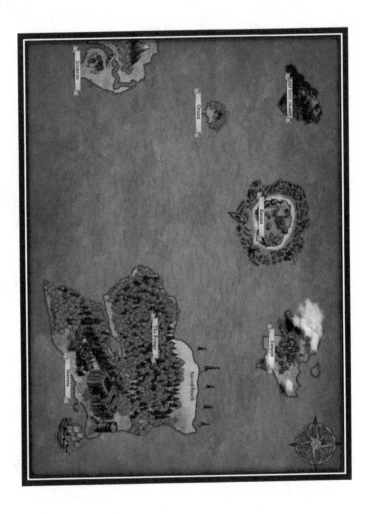

Chapter 1

"Mist rolls off the sea and creeps through every corner and crevice of a small fishing town. From the steeple bell to the pub's cold liquor storage room, the little island is consumed by a thick, ghostly fog. All the children are fast asleep, the pub locals have stumbled home and the moon has reached its highest peak and fullest form. It will come deep in the night, without warning, without time for preparation and without prevention. The few who have survived say you can hear a low drumbeat in the distance before it happens. This sleepy village will become victim to Lord Demetrius, Captain of *Hades Pride*, conqueror of the sea and king of Lost Soul Island!" Jeremiah springs forward towards the other kids as the last words jump out of his mouth in a growl. His story sends them screaming playfully around the cargo hold of a transport ship. They each have small pieces of driftwood, used as swords to act out the rest of the gruesome story. Jeremiah is the oldest of the five children at seventeen and one half. A handsome boy, wiser than his age with black hair and a fit physique

"Oh, Captain De-meee-trius," a smaller girl sings behind Jeremiah. He spins to face her just as she swings her stick at his chest. Jeremiah deflects the stick with his 'sword'.

"It's Lord Demetrius, you dimwitted girl! Into a volcanic doom with you!" He picks the girl up, a small task with her petite figure, and tosses her into a pile of rope and mops. The girl is quickly back on her feet, grabbing another piece of wood and challenging a boy more her size. She strikes the other boy hard on his side and he attacks back with the butt end of his 'sword' into her shoulder. The boy, Keedo, is not much of a battle for the girl. He meets the ground in the blink of an eye from a quick placement of her heel to his back foot. Her fast strikes and advanced form make her a difficult opponent even for Jeremiah.

The children are being held captive in the cargo hold of a ship belonging to the Command. They have each been sold to the slave trade and are off to the island of Varthia, headquarters of the Command. Here, their fate lies at an auction where they are sold off like cattle to the highest bidder. Each of the slave children has their story — whether it is a brush with Command, their masters no longer need them, or their own parents sell them for a small coin. This is Jeremiah's second time journeying to Varthia.

"What did you do this time, Jer?" asks the girl Jeremiah sent flying into a volcanic doom, moments earlier. Her name is Quinn, and this wasn't the first time Jeremiah had voyaged a slave trade route with her. He guesses she is about sixteen. Her long, golden and matted hair dances around her small figure like curtains, guarding something precious. From their previous pretends, he knows that she is surprisingly strong considering her size. Jeremiah imagines she grew up on the streets of a poor island where sheer living conditioned her to be a competitive opponent. A matter of survival of the fittest. They made a pact on one of their first nights together long ago to never tell where they came from. Instead, they fantasized pasts as an escape from the desolate world they know as a reality. Jeremiah, the rich and glorified contract hero, journeying to Varthia on a secret Command mission. Quinn, a warrior princess who was caught stealing a fishing boat for her small village.

"The Command asked me back to help fight off a giant now that I've gotten more muscular. I'm sure the Varthian capital will have a feast in my honour — you'd be lucky to attend." Jeremiah flexes his arms and flashes a full smile at her. In truth, Varthia couldn't afford even a small parade since they began wars with Lord Demetrius years ago, making the once great capital a third world country. He doesn't have to explain his reasoning though and she doesn't ask. Instead, she smiles brightly at him, happy to play along with their game. Quinn rolls her eyes and runs to challenge Keedo again who is getting tired of being beaten by a girl. Watching her send Keedo to the ground in a single motion is impressive to say the least. She catches

Jeremiah's longing glances and laughs aloud as a face-down Keedo struggles to get out from underneath her grip.

Jeremiah looks over at the other two girls, decorating their 'swords' with rope and other items they gathered from inside the cargo hold. The youngest is named Scotty. He knows she is only eleven since her older sister Syd keeps reminding everyone. Syd's age is a mystery, but he guesses her to be approaching adulthood. This is the first night the girls have stopped crying since they joined them in the cargo hold nearly a week prior.

"Are you just going to keep staring at us or are we going to play?" Scotty asks Jeremiah teasingly. Jeremiah must have spaced out in his thoughts, but quickly recovers.

"I would never dream of harming a princess. I shall capture you and hold a ransom over your head!" Jeremiah darts towards them. Sydney shakes her head at his pretend act, too mature for childish games, and continues to braid rope around her stick. Scotty on the other hand starts playfully running away. Her bare feet barely make a sound as she skips around the cargo hold.

"You can't catch me, you nasty Tipray!" Scotty shouts teasingly. Sydney gasps at her sister and begins scolding her for using the name. You see, Tipray was the God who caused the waters to rise and take over the lands, killing millions of people and leaving only small islands surrounded by oceans. Scotty pays no attention to her nagging sister, too busy giggling at Jeremiah's cat and mouse game. He inches closer and closer to the little girl, causing her to forget their surroundings and squeal loudly at the enjoyment of the game.

"Shush!" Jeremiah exclaims as he puts his hand over the little girl's mouth. An eleven-year-old's scream carries much further than a little giggling. She panics at his grip and instinctually bites down on his hand, but he doesn't loosen his hold.

The floorboards above them creak. Someone is coming.

"Stop!" Jeremiah commands with urgency in his voice. He lets go of Scotty and hurries everyone into their sleeping places. Broken scraps of old sails on the ground make up beds for the children. Jeremiah closes his eyes in his own sleeping place just as he hears the jingle of a key in the lock above. A hook grabs onto the cargo hold's large grate door, opening with a creak of rusty hinges from years of saltwater exposure. The ladder's steps moan with every movement made by the newcomer on the way down. Jeremiah keeps his eyes closed and concentrates on his breathing. Deep breath in and a slow breath out in a rhythmic fashion as if he is in a deep sleep. Scotty's teeth marks are stinging on his hand and Jeremiah can feel the wetness of blood. He hurries the pain out of his mind, so he can concentrate on the newcomer walking about the cargo hold. A deep sense of responsibility has been on his shoulders since he arrived on the ship. Not only a pressure he has put on himself to protect them, but an unspoken expectation from the other children. His mind concentrates now, and he can sense the man's presence. Jeremiah hears a click between each step that makes the hairs on the back of his neck rise. It's Cookie and his walking stick that was jimmy-rigged from an old mast. The smell of rum and body odor fills the small room which is saying a lot considering the children haven't left the cargo hold in a week. Their bathroom bucket hasn't been dumped in a few days and the newcomer's stench still overpowers the smell. It would be an awful confrontation if Cookie caught Jeremiah awake. Rum and too much saltwater does something to a man's mind. The footsteps stop at the starboard side of the cargo hold. Jeremiah opens one eye slowly to see Cookie drop his drawers, remove his manhood and take a leak on the floor. What a waste of a man, Jeremiah thinks to himself. Every inch of him is repulsive. His boots are mismatched and rotting, there are only a handful of hairs that inhabit his head and gingivitis has burrowed deeply in his mouth. The Tradey lets out a burp and begins humming an old Varthian song used to put children to sleep. It's incredible that he can stand let alone maneuver a ladder. Cookie pulls his shorts up and changes his madman humming to an eerie whistle mixed with singing and the occasional hiccup.

"Blue and Black are hung at our mast,

We vow to serve and protect our Sea." *Hiccup*.

He begins walking beside all the children, carefully inspecting each of them. 'Please don't do anything stupid' Jeremiah thinks.

"Though the waters continue to rise fast,

To our posts, we'll always be." *Hiccup*.

Cookie limps his way over to the girls' side of the room and stops his walking and singing. He stares down at them with his back towards Jeremiah who has a sharpened piece of wood that he keeps in his leather belt. Clutching the weapon tightly, he slowly raises his body in preparation to strike. The drunk Tradey breathes in deep and fast which makes Jeremiah's stomach rise into his throat. Cookie makes the abnormal breathing noise again and lets out a loud, "Ah-choo!" followed by sniffling. The drunk Tradey starts walking back towards the rotting ladder, satisfied with his inspection of the child captives. Jeremiah realizes he's been holding his breath since Cookie waddled down the steps. He breathes out heavily as he hears the grate door close with a slam.

"Drunk Tradies," Jeremiah breathes out as he hears the other men greet Cookie back on deck and begin singing the rest of the Varthian anthem in tone deaf unison. Tradies are hired peddlers that are paid off in a small amount of coin and a large amount of liquor by the Varthian Command. It is easier to control a drunken man used to a life begging on the streets than a man looking to earn an honest wage. That being said, most of the Tradies are taken as children and put through the child slave trade until they are of age. If they reach the age of eighteen and are still slaves to the rich, they can be sold at twice their regular rate or are immediately initiated into the Tradey world by the governing militia, the Command. They are cleaned and branded with the Command's symbol; the Crystal Star that rests directly above Varthia with swords crossing behind. It signifies their life belonging to the Command. Even the lowest ranked Varthian official can order them about with penalty of death for the slightest disobedience. Cookie's mark is on his right wrist. When the emblem is on the left wrist, it means that person is pure evil. Rapists, murderers and pedophiles get this mark. The Command has been preying on peddlers and children this way for as long as anyone can remember. They send Tradies to uncivilized islands that are not governed by the Command with the sole purpose of buying women and children for resale in Varthia. Tradies who work with human transport are better off than the others. They get full meals, all the rum their bellies can handle and female company when they return to Varthia. Other Tradies get stuck on fishing boats or voyages for months under an officer's watch, get selected for building projects in Varthia, or the worst is working directly for an officer of the Command. At least Tradies like Cookie don't have the Command breathing down their neck when they are far out in the waters, treacherous as they can be. Jeremiah's sympathy for Tradies wore thin after being used as human target practice on his first journey to Varthia. His fingers graze the scar on his right shoulder from where the new Tradey nicked him with the rusty dagger. An involuntary snarl escaped from his mouth at the thought. What kind of people use a twelve-year-old kid as an initiation tactic? They are the scum of the central waters. They deserve to be oppressed by the Command with all the disrespect and mistreatment that goes with it.

*****

Jeremiah's thoughts start fading as he rolls over and begins to fall into his in-between. This is where he gets to see her. She is running through the trees in a dense meadow. Not darting between the trees, but running inside them, running through them.   With   each disappearing act, she laughs with the innocence of a child, always looking in Jeremiah's direction. This is his favorite in-between. She has skin that resembles the trees in colour and texture, but smoother. Her hair seems to be dancing with the wind in a ferocity contradicting her steady ocean blue eyes. Her smile brings him the deepest peace he has ever felt. She silences the demons that are determined to break him. She makes him feel like a child in the simplest, most innocent form. He reaches out for her, but she dodges his touch. He tries again, but she dodges him once more, like a dog with its toy. Frustration and anger fill Jeremiah with every reach that comes back empty. Even the slightest graze of his

17

finger on a single strand of her hair would satisfy. She dodges his advances faster as Jeremiah becomes more enraged and furious with every passing second. Suddenly, the skies become dark and the woman's face goes from laughter to terror. Jeremiah feels wetness on his skin; he rubs his cheek and looks at his hand. It's not rain, it's thick and red — blood. The woman runs toward him, crying out to him. He can't understand what she is saying.

A dark figure appears above him. There is too much of a shadow to see who or what it is. The figure steps into view and reaches out to grab Jeremiah. Suddenly, he wakes with a jolt. He is soaked with sweat, no, it's rain. The skies that were once clear have been consumed with black clouds. A rush of water pours into the cargo hold, waking the other children up.

Quinn runs towards Jeremiah and slaps him into reality, a full hand across his face.

"Snap out of it Jer, we need to get out of here before she takes us under." Quinn shakes his shoulders then runs off to wake Keedo.

Jeremiah closes his eyes and imagines the woman's smile again. The damp grass between his toes, the smell of the blue flowers in the wind and the sun beaming down on him. Another wave of salty water comes crashing in from the cargo hold, directly into his mouth. Jeremiah coughs out the salty water and stands up slowly. He grabs onto the side of the ship to get balance as the angered waves shove the ship back and forth. A thought hits him while holding on for dear life — did Cookie lock the cargo hold? He tries to remember if he heard the key jingle in the lock, but there is only one way to find out.

"Quinn! The dumb bastard didn't lock up!" he yells across the cargo hold.

Quinn looks confused at first, almost like she doesn't understand or didn't hear him. Jeremiah makes a locking motion with his hands and points at the grate door above. Quinn smiles brightly at first and then points down at broken shards of wood that were once the ladder, floating in the fast-rising water. The hope drains from Jeremiah's eyes. He sees the ladder that once connected them to their freedom is now in pieces. By the time the water rises enough to reach the grate door, the ship will already be in her watery grave.

Drunk Tradies yell muffled commands to each other above, a futile effort to keep the ship afloat. The water has risen to Jeremiah's waist, now. He holds both hands in his thick black hair, trying to squeeze a plan from his foggy mind. Think, Jeremiah, think. He can hear the Tradies above him, yelling at each other in drunken slur.

"Jer, what are you doing? You can't give up now!" Quinn yells in frustration. "Jer, answer me!"

Keedo is swimming around the cargo hold, looking for a way to escape. He is a surprisingly good swimmer, taking long dives between breaths.

Syd is comforting her sobbing sister, holding onto a floating crate. "It will be okay, Scotty, we will get out of here."

A loud *CRACK* breaks the chaos and the once barely afloat transport comes to a halt. "LAND HO!" one of the pirates calls from above. The ship creaks and groans in pain from the hit. Water rushes even faster into the cargo hold from below them. Jeremiah holds his breath and swims down to assess the damage. A rock has punctured a small hole in the hull. The force of the ship against the rock is ripping the hole bigger and bigger. It will soon be enough space for a person to get through. Jeremiah sees Keedo is looking in his direction and motions for him to swim back to the surface of the cargo hold. The kids look to Jeremiah for a plan. That unspoken expectation of responsibility is heavy on Jeremiah's sinking shoulders.

"Scotty, there's enough space right now for you to swim through the hole first. Quinn, you will go next, followed by Sydney, Keedo and then me," Jeremiah instructs them.

"I can't hold my breath that long!" Syd protests with terror in her eyes.

"She has to hold her nose, my pa never taught her," Scotty informs them. Syd shoots daggers at her sister, feeling betrayed that her weakness was revealed. Jeremiah views it as a waste of emotion with danger so imminent but doesn't show his disapproval. He swims over to Syd, grabbing her hand to guide her off the crate in preparation for the dive under.

"You have to be strong right now. Your sister needs you. If you hold your nose, you won't give yourself enough swimming strength to make it out. I'm going to go help Scotty and Quinn get out while Keedo waits with you and then we are going to get out, okay?" Sydney nods her head in trembling understanding.

Jeremiah motions to Quinn and Scotty. "On the count of three, one... two... three!" Jeremiah takes a deep breath and leads the girls to the hull, hurrying them along as the water is quickly filling the boat, sinking them further under. He kicks more of the wooden hull around the rock and Scotty squeezes through with ease. Quinn touches Jeremiah's cheek before swimming to the opening and squeezing her way around the rock. She nicks her knee slightly but is out and away in the blink of an eye. Jeremiah swims back to the surface where Keedo and Sydney are waiting. Tears run down Sydney's cheeks in between short, terror-filled breaths.

"Get it together, Syd, think about your favorite memory... your sister... anything except for how much this scares you. You need to control your fear right now." He grabs her hand and leads her once again away from her safety crate. "We are going under on the count of three. One... two..." *CRACK*. The sound of the rock tearing more out of the hull cuts Jeremiah's countdown short. Water rushes in like millions of little ocean soldiers, determined to bring the ship down before they can escape. The force of the water creates an undertow, aggressively pulling them towards the hole in the hull. Jeremiah and Keedo grab onto the side of the ship and wait for the force of the water to slow down. Jeremiah opens his eyes underwater and looks around for Sydney. He can't see her but can hear her screaming. Her body gets dragged and tossed in front of them towards the hole. Jeremiah reaches out to grab her hand, but her foot gets caught in rope causing her head to slam into the hull. Jeremiah watches in horror as her body goes limp and waves rhythmically with the rushing water. It's the most peaceful he's ever seen her. The wrinkle in her brow where she kept her worry, smooths. She looks like a child once more. Keedo grabs Jeremiah's arm and begins to lead him towards the hole, away from Sydney's lifeless body.

Jeremiah shakes Keedo's grip and swims back to get her. He easily releases her body from the rope and pushes her towards the hole, towards their escape. Keedo grabs her arms and guides her through the hole before disappearing into the abyss. Jeremiah needs to take a breath, but the water is all the way to the top of the cargo hold now. He darts toward the hole and squeezes his body through. It's a tight fit, but his body is out. Suddenly, the boat shifts again, and Jeremiah's foot is caught between the rock and hull. Pain rushes from his foot throughout the rest of his body. 'I'm going to die here' he thinks. He looks back at his foot that is jammed between the rock and the hull of the ship.

Tugging, pulling, twisting and pushing, nothing is working. His foot is stuck. 'Is this where it ends?' His chest is in pain from holding his breath so long. He can hear his heart beat faster and faster, taking over his thoughts, and a solemn realization begins to set in. Jeremiah relaxes his body and looks around at the world that will become his tomb. The orphan boy who no one wants, and no one will miss, drowned at the bottom of the ocean. He could have escaped if he hadn't helped the others, but of course this thought doesn't occur to him until he is looking death in the face. Jeremiah closes his eyes and makes one last futile pull with his leg — it frees. He looks at his foot and it's no longer stuck. Confusion, excitement and panic hit him all at once. He swims as hard and fast as he can to the top, inhaling water on the way up. It feels like a thousand meters to the surface, but he makes it and gasps for as much air as his lungs can handle. Salt water spews out of his mouth, releasing pressure from his chest. Fresh air never tasted so good.

He reaches for a floating crate to hold onto while rubbing the salt water out of his eyes. It's just occurred to him how cold the water is. Both the rain and waves have found peace with the world now. Jeremiah looks up at the grey clouds to see a hazy morning sun slowly peeking through. As he brings his gaze down, he sees the outline of land in the distance. He closes his eyes and lets the drift of the water carry his body towards the island of Varthia.

Chapter 2

A golden beach runs along the northern side of Varthia, inhabited only by hungry seagulls and happy crabs scouring for their next meal. Giant wooden stakes and warning signs have been placed out in the water to prohibit unwanted visitors from landing on the sacred beach. Even the locals living in Varthia are forbidden from walking the sandy oasis. This summer morning, the sea has offered an unexpected, yet welcomed menu for the seagulls. An appetizer, entrée and dessert of washed-up scraps from a Tradey transport ship. Their caws lull a passed-out Jeremiah from his almost comatose state. He can feel the water rushing up to his neck with each wave that comes rolling onto the sandy beach. The rhythmic sound of the crashing waves brings him memories of his first home on the island of Knoen. He squints his eyes open against the harsh sun and is comforted when he sees the sea carried him onto the abandoned shore and not on the other side of the island where the Varthian city stands in all its cold, black glory. Next to him is a man dressed in garments consistent with Tradey garb. An old Varthian uniform jacket with holes where the patches would have been, one-size-fits-all pants and generic leather boots. The

Tradey's face takes on the pale green colour of a recently drowned man. If it wasn't the colour of his skin, it would be the light stench of decay that indicated this Tradey didn't survive the wreck. Sitting up takes all the will power inside of Jeremiah, but he knows he needs to move. A Varthian Command patrol will be looking for survivors, soon. Slave kids bring the Command funding through trade primarily, but they also get turned into Tradey workers once they hit eighteen. You don't want to be in Varthia when you are of age. Jeremiah once had a young Tradey transport worker tell him of the torturous treatment involved in the Tradey training camp. They treat the young slaves as horses requiring to be broken from free-spirited bucking broncos to an obedient steed. The thought of spending a lifetime working for the Varthian Command sends shivers up Jeremiah's spine. He slides the dead Tradey's jacket off his lifeless body and gently pulls the man's boots off his feet.

He's missing a few toes which doesn't strike Jeremiah as odd since he's encountered his share of torture from the Command and Tradies themselves.

His hazy memory of the night before slowly creeps its way back into his mind. The shipwreck, the other children and Quinn. He frantically twists his body and head around looking for signs of Quinn and the others. A horrible thought punches Jeremiah in the gut. What if they got caught by Varthian Command soldiers? What fate would fall upon them? He pushes those thoughts away. Quinn would be smart enough to move inland to the hundreds of kilometers of forest between the beach and Varthian's city wall. He rolls onto his side to stand up, but pain stops him halfway. His ankle gives out, sitting him back onto the sand and shooting pain from his foot to his stomach. It is discolored and swollen, but he is certain there is no break as he wiggles his toes with ease. He slides the drowned Tradey's leather boots on carefully to avoid irritating his already sore ankle. A size too big, but he ties them tight and wiggles his toes in them, admiring how foreign they feel on his usually bare feet. Spotting a large rock inland, he army-crawls towards the forest and maneuvers himself to a standing position. The pain causes him to wince as he slowly puts weight on the injury but judges he can at least limp about. He looks out at the water that he once thought would be his tomb. The sky is clear of the thunderous rainclouds and the water has changed to a calm blue. You could never have guessed that a vicious storm overtook the waters mere hours before. A school of flying fish jump out of the water, catching Jeremiah's eye. He has always been mesmerized by their brilliant purple and blue colors. Each couple inside the pod has a choreographed dance in and outside the water. The fish's length is only about one and a half meters, but they can easily soar three times that out of the water with their dragon-like wings reaching far and wide. At the peak of their bound, they close their wings making a tuck-and-roll motion back into the water with hardly a splash. A light in the water catches his eye in between the fifth and sixth couple of fish. There is something else inside the water with the pod. He picks a Mactro flower to get a better view. The long, bulky stem acts as a telescope through the magnified blue flower at the tip. He scans the water to find the pod again and gets a better view of the creature. It's much bigger than the flying fish, but it has joined in almost flawlessly with their dance. The creature has two long deep blue fins that are reflecting the sunlight. Jeremiah tries to catch a glimpse of the head but it's too far away and quickly swimming out of sight. They are just about to swim out of view when the creatures turn to make the jump out of the water. Jeremiah aims his telescopic flower at the point of penetration and catches a much better view of the creature. It's not like any fish head he's seen, in fact, it looks almost human. He takes the Mactro away and rubs his eyes. He must still have saltwater in them.

CRACK. Jeremiah feels pain on the back of his head and his bright world becomes dark once again.

Chapter 3

Jeremiah's mind brings him back to his first home of Knoen in a vivid in-between. Raised 1,000 meters above sea level and surrounded by 3,000 meters of dense reef, it's no wonder the Command chose this island to protect their history in the form of thousands of old books, relics and treasures. Many reefs in the sea are living, breathing creatures, but the reef around Knoen was created with particularly evil intentions. Hidden throughout a black maze of toxic reef lies hundreds of crevices that open and close like mouths, breathing in the poisonous air above and waiting for the next meal to fall in. The edges of these chasms are surrounded by sharp teeth-like rocks, easily swallowing a man whole. When the two days of low tide hit, hundreds of bones and shipwrecked skeletons are revealed like a sea graveyard. Some sailors have come across maps that claim to get you through the maze, but no one has been successful. Even if you came across such a map, you'd still have to make it past the reef roamers. Once humans lived on the island but were forced into drinking the reef's water and eating the anemone's poisonous tongues by the Varthian Command, their skin turned a dark blue, the reef grew on their body and their fingers and toes started forming into fins. They changed so much into sea creatures that the reef recognized them as its own being. Cannibalistic in nature with a vindictive taste for human flesh, they long for wanderers to coax into a torturous fate. The Varthian Command chose this island specifically for the natural defense, so they could store their world's history without fear of it being taken or destroyed. Nearly one hundred years ago they built the Librae and placed holy men to defend the historic documents protected inside. These men called Ascetics vowed to protect not only the books, but the history written in them. They dedicated their lives to learning and memorizing the stories. One Ascetic, against his better judgement, dedicated a small portion of his life to raising a child.

Jeremiah didn't remember a life before this place. He lived with the groundskeeper, Anuva, and spent his evenings reading all about the Gods, the history of the Command and the evil Lord Demetrius. Tasked with keeping the Ascetics happy by cooking, cleaning, keeping the grounds looking beautiful and tending to the various farm animals, Jeremiah led a simply yet busy childhood. The horses were his favorite. There was something poetic about a force so unaware of their own power and ability to be free of their reins. He also had a knack for gardening. Like an ogre in the history books, he was born with a green thumb. Twelve years as the only young person among adults like the Ascetics gave Jeremiah a maturity unmeasurable to children his age, but he didn't know any different nor was he told otherwise. Days and weeks were lost getting into trouble on the island through pranks and annoying the Ascetics, but also sneaking into the Librae to tame his mountain-sized desire for knowledge. The reality of being stuck on an island for your entire life with no means of entertainment aside from imagination seemed grave to him when he was young. He dreamed of worlds far away, but his vast training with the Ascetics painted a different future for him. Perspective is a strange creature.

Anuva is in Jeremiah's in-between. They are back on the grassy island, watching the sun set in the distance while a twelve-year-old Jeremiah reads his favorite book — the story of Lillius, Deity of the earth. Within these pages, Lillius saved the humans from the rising waters by sacrificing her own freedom, leaving behind the islands like Varthia and Knoen for people to live on. Jeremiah doesn't know if he believes in the Gods, but he finds the stories fascinating.

"We have hundreds of books that you have yet to read, my boy, why do you always choose this one?" Anuva probes the boy, partially out of habit, but more to assess his current mood.

"I like this story best. I like to think she would die before giving me up," Jeremiah says with underlying resentment dripping from every word.

"It's not up to me, Jeremiah. Isaar knows best. The Command is giving us more books they found, and we are not supposed to have children here permanently.

One of the other Ascetics slipped in speaking to a member of the Command and mentioned your existence. You must go with them back to Varthia. It's out of my hands, Jeremiah." Anuva wishes he could explain. He tries to reason with the boy, but he knows he cannot ease the abandonment. Especially to an orphan. Jeremiah chokes down a lump in his throat. He looks over the edge of the raised island. The Tradey boat anchored beyond the reef.   The pulley system in the distance squeals in distress, bringing the Command captain, his precious books and Jeremiah's desolate fate. This will be his last evening with Anuva and he can't bring himself to even look at the only father figure he's ever known. No, he wants to, but he chooses not to.

"I better go and pack my belongings." Jeremiah shuts the book and caresses the soft leather cover.

"I scripted a copy of the book to take with you. It's sitting on your pillow." Anuva reaches to touch the boy, but Jeremiah pulls away and walks towards their shack. A one room shelter made of mud and straw only for sleeping and hiding out bad weather.

It only takes ten paces before the boy turns back where Anuva stands with his back to the boy, facing the ocean. Jeremiah wants to yell at Anuva, he wants to know why he is letting Isaar trade him for some books. Anuva remains with his back to Jeremiah, keeping his focus on the setting sun. Jeremiah goes to speak, but a strong wind comes, almost blowing him over into the yellow grass. Tears well in his eyes as he runs to the

31

shack. Inside their small hut, he finds the scripted book, just as Anuva promised, lying on his pillow.

To Jeremiah,
May knowledge find you and wisdom guide you.
Anuva

The most common, unemotional phrase among Ascetics with as much depth as a sneeze. This is how he says goodbye? Is this all I'm worth to him? A tear rolls from duct to cheek and onto the daggered words. He starts ripping the pages out of the book in a reactive fit of rage. Page after page, he not only tears them out of the well fastened binding but shreds them with his hands and teeth like a crazed lion and its prey. The world becomes blurry with tears as he falls onto his straw bed surrounded by the destroyed pages. The pages telling a story of a God who sacrificed himself for Jeremiah's freedom when the only father Jeremiah has known will see him taken far away to the Varthian slave trade for some old books. The rage grows deeper and deeper inside, gasoline on fire. Jeremiah glances in a broken mirror to see his eyes turning from a blue colour to jet black. He puts his hands to his ears and begins screaming. The scream changes from childlike piercing to an aggressive roar. Hurricane strength winds escape from inside him and spray out of his mouth, swirling the pages around the hut. His feet leave the ground as he is lifted, hovering over his bed. The shack shakes from the strength of his cry. Pieces of the hut begin circling with the pages of the book. Paper and debris float in the wind coming from Jeremiah. Before the whole hut crumbles to the ground, he hits his head on the ceiling, breaking the gales to nothing and dropping him back onto the straw bed. His eyes turn back to their sky blue and Jeremiah stares at the wooden ceiling, counting backwards to calm down just like Anuva taught him the last time he lost control.

"Five, four, three… two… one."

Chapter 4

"Wake up, kid." A deep elderly voice jerks Jeremiah from out of his in-between in a panic.

"Is he dead?" A child's voice asks.

"He sure talks in his sleep a lot to be dead, stupid!" an older child lectures, condescendingly.

Jeremiah opens his eyes to three faces looking curiously at him. He swallows hard and licks his dry lips. A strong pain on his head brings him to reality, making him feel nauseous.

"He lives!" said the elderly man, putting a coconut cup to Jeremiah's lips. He drinks the liquid welcomingly and without hesitation. He can't even remember the last time he quenched his thirst. They are rationed on the Tradey transport and he gave most of his share to the younger children.

The man takes the cup away and turns to set it on a wooden cabinet. Jeremiah slowly reaches for the weapon in his pants, but finds he is completely naked underneath a burlap blanket. He reaches towards the source of his pain on the back of his head, but finds it is wrapped in some kind of fabric. His hand is also bandaged from where Scotty bit him on the ship.

"Where am I?" Jeremiah asks, feeling and sounding groggy. He starts sitting up, but finds his waist and ankles are restrained to the wooden bed. Panic sets in and the elderly man recognizes it instantly.

"Easy now, we wouldn't want you running away on us," the man says with a smile. "You certainly do dream a lot." He begins shooing the children out of the small room and locks the wooden door behind them.

Jeremiah's heart is pounding loudly into his head. He twists his upper body and neck to take in his surroundings. Dark earth walls and ceiling indicate he is in some type of underground room. There are no windows, only candles to bring them light. A broken mirror to the left of Jeremiah reveals dark scruff on his face which draws his uncovered hand instantly to it, scratching and playing with the beard. He's never been allowed to grow out his facial hair. It makes him look much older. The beard had been growing since he had been on the transport ship and would have been cut off had he made it to the Varthian capital.

There are no pictures or other furniture in the room aside from his bed and the wooden cabinet. The entry door seems to be the only way out, but first he must get these restraints off. He tries to pull the leather bands off his waist, but they appear to be fastened underneath the bed where his reach ends. The man shakes his head at Jeremiah's efforts and walks toward the cabinet again, grabbing a wooden bowl off a shelf and filling it with liquid. He brings the bowl towards Jeremiah and sets it on the bed. He then reaches towards the bandages on Jeremiah's head, but is met with resistance. Jeremiah reaches out and pushes the man's hand away. A stern frown and wrinkled brow indicate his disapproval of Jeremiah's reaction.

"It doesn't matter to me, young man. You can let it rot or I can clean it, but I am too old and too tired to fight you." He reaches towards a speechless Jeremiah again, but this time is permitted to adjust his bandages. The elderly man gets the cloth off completely with a slight struggle at the end as the blood from Jeremiah's wound has dried to the cloth. A long time goes by as the man puts on a broken pair of spectacles, cleans Jeremiah's head wound and runs a needle and thread through it. A wince escapes Jeremiah's mouth every few seconds from the pain, but no other conversation occurs.

Jeremiah stares at the old man, feeling less groggy now. It is a rare occurrence to meet someone so old. Elderly people are not useful on the thirty-nine islands governed by the Command and are usually killed off to save rations for the young and strong.

"Where am I?" Jeremiah asks for the second time.

"Best not to ask questions, my boy. The less you know the more likely you can leave this place alive," says the old man.

"Can you at least tell me your name? I'd like to thank you properly," Jeremiah asks, hoping to gain the old man's trust. He searches the man's face for a change in expression.

"You may call me Cornelius. That's enough talking for now," he replies with a stern tone.

Jeremiah studies the man carefully. He judges Cornelius at a slouched six feet with a bigger build, showing signs he was a strong man once. He wouldn't describe him as frail, but aged with grey, tired eyes. Walking around the room, Jeremiah notices he has a slight limp, favoring his right knee. The few grey hairs Cornelius has left on his head are combed over as if giving the illusion that he isn't balding. The old man tests Jeremiah's reflexes, eyesight and speech to ensure brain damage is not a concern. Jeremiah remembers reading about doctors in Knoen's Librae but never experienced such an examination. It's no wonder Cornelius wasn't killed off. Doctors are a hard find in these times. Although, Jeremiah isn't certain he is in Varthian's city. They structure their buildings consistent with their castle. Cold black stone and concrete; not mud and earth. Even Varthian's underground jail cells are lined with the black stone.

"Are we in Varthia?" Jeremiah decides to ask. What's the worst that could happen?

Cornelius sighs heavily. "I said no questions." He gathers the bloody cloths and puts them in a brown bag. Then, he walks over to the wooden cabinet and dips the needle into a jar of liquid. "We are on the island of

Varthia, yes," Cornelius says, answering Jeremiah's question despite his attempts at silence.

Why would he distinguish we are on the island and not say the city or just Varthia? Jeremiah decides to push his luck just a little bit further. "Are we in the Fringe?"

Cornelius peers at Jeremiah over his broken glasses, realizing he's said too much. A knock at the door breaks their eye contact and sends Jeremiah's stomach into his throat.

"Is the detainee ready, yet?" a woman's voice asks from the door.

"Give us two more minutes, Trish," Cornelius responds.

"Come on, old man. He was supposed to be ready an hour ago for trial," the female voice complains.

"Did she just say trial?" Jeremiah whispers to Cornelius.

His question is ignored as Cornelius hands him a pair of torn pants and a large white shirt. He helps Jeremiah put the shirt on and unhooks the restraints. Cornelius then turns silently, giving the boy privacy for dressing. Jeremiah slides one leg at a time into the ragged pants. He stands to pull them up and tie with a rope belt. The pain in his ankle is barely noticeable any more, but his head starts spinning like a top. Cornelius turns around just in time to catch Jeremiah from falling over.

"Easy now, boy. The water I gave you was soaked with Rekelp and will ease the pain while you go through the trial. The effect should take place very soon and I'll give you another dose if you come back to my care," Cornelius explains.

"If?" A concerned and confused Jeremiah asks.

"Come on, Cornelius, or the Appointed will have both our heads," Trish shouts while impatiently banging on the door.

Jeremiah re-focuses his eyes and scrounges up enough willpower to stand without Cornelius's help. Once he regains his balance, he turns to the man and whispers, "Thank you."

Cornelius looks apprehensive as he stares into Jeremiah's eyes, searching for answers to questions he hasn't asked. "Take this," he says, handing Jeremiah a small, but sharp, carving knife. "I don't know why you were on the beach, but these people aren't going to treat you nicely. You may have seen too much, but I believe you are not here to cause any harm. I believe you were at the wrong place at the wrong time."

Jeremiah opens his mouth to ask a hundred questions, but Cornelius walks to the door before he can form even one. Jeremiah quickly shoves the knife into a small pocket in his pants as Cornelius unlocks the door and opens it for Trish, the impatient. She is a very fit woman with a boyish figure, dark skin and long black hair tied in a loose braid. Her black eyes pierce right through Jeremiah as if she were a king and he a mere peasant. Although she is very stunning, there is nothing about her that Jeremiah would describe as feminine. From her stern features to her strong body, she is as gentle as a rabid dog. She grabs Jeremiah's arms, putting them in front of him and locks iron circles around them. Then, she places her hand on Jeremiah's shoulder and shoves him forward through the door.

Even with the irons on his wrists, not knowing where he is going or what he is being tried for, Jeremiah feels relieved. He isn't being traded in Varthia and he isn't a slave to the Command. For once in his life, his path isn't clear, isn't laid out in front of him and isn't in the Tradey's control. He is… free.

Chapter 5

"Pick up the pace, kid," Trish demands, shoving Jeremiah again.

He walks down a long corridor with Trish bringing up the rear and shoving him forward every ten paces. The corridor is enclosed like the room with a half dozen more rooms extending out from the hall. A sharp left turn offers more natural light coming from ahead. The underground corridor turns into a cavern with four-meter walls and an open ceiling. Sunlight blazes in through the trees above and a strong sea wind blows towards them. He breathes in deeply, standing still to feel the warmth of the sun on his face and the fresh air in his lungs. Jeremiah hasn't felt direct sunlight since… he doesn't even know. How long was he knocked out in that room? Trish shoves Jeremiah again, breaking his thoughts. He looks back at Trish to show his disapproval of her manners before walking again. The carving knife grazes his side in his pocket, incessantly reminding him of its presence. He hopes Trish doesn't see it. They pass around another corner to reveal more roofless caverns, but this time the walls are lined with what appears to be bones in the walls. Skeletons, complete with skulls, tucked into the walls like a catacomb. He stops to examine what he thought was an empty hole, but the bones were simply too small to see at first glance. What kind of place is this? Trish's hand reaches up and pushes him forward again.

"Are you always this pleasant with visitors?" Jeremiah asks Trish sarcastically, trying to gauge his transporter's demeanor.

"Only with Tradey spies," Trish retaliates after a few moments of silence, followed up by another shove forward.

No wonder they've been locking Jeremiah up. He's on his way to court to be tried as a spy! He thinks long and hard about his next response. Being surrounded by catacombs makes him cautious of his words as they will determine his fate.

"What if I told you I was in Tradey transport and not a spy?" Jeremiah asks Trish calmly.

"A transport? Ha!" A forced laugh with offensive intentions. "The only way you could be a transport is if you were a kid. You might want to think of a different story for the Appointed. You don't look a day younger than twenty-five. Not to mention I found you snooping around the Fringe in Tradey wear." She pushes him forward again.

Jeremiah touches the back of his head, remembering how he was hit at the beach and now knowing it was Trish who packed the blow. He decides its best not to respond to her any further. He doesn't know what kind of people he is dealing with. They could be savages who would kill him if they thought he was a useless transport. He's heard tales of the Fringe people before, but thought them nothing but rumors designed by the Command to deter the Varthian people from trying to escape, leading them all to believe they were lunatics and cannibals. Judging by the skeletons still lining the walls, there may be truth to the rumors. Trish and Jeremiah round another sharp corner in the cavern. Green vines with exotic pink flowers begin to line the stone walls. A welcome transition from the death lined catacombs. The floors are covered with soft earth and red sand, tickling his bare feet as he walks through. A large wooden door with rusty fixtures lies at the end of the cavern. There are old, worn out words carved into the stone around the door, but Jeremiah can't make out what they say. Trish walks to it and knocks in a sequence of two light and quick knocks followed by another three hard, closed-fist pounds, much like the impatient knocks at Cornelius's room. A chill of anticipation crawls its way up Jeremiah's back. The door opens with a creak revealing nothing but darkness inside. A female voice calls out from within, "Bring in the prisoner." Jeremiah both anticipates and dodges Trish's push from behind and smiles playfully at her before being consumed by the darkness beyond the entrance.

Chapter 6

Whispers meet Jeremiah's ears first as he enters the dark room. It takes a few seconds, but his eyes start to adjust to the dim lighting. Quickly, he realizes he is in the middle of a small arena style room, in the same underground theme. It is an oval shape with a chair directly in the middle and four rows full of people surrounding him in stadium seating, all with grueling faces looking down at him. A tinted glass ceiling changes the naturally bright sun to an ominous blue, setting a chilling tone for his trial. He wonders what the glass ceiling would look like from above. How have they hidden this catacomb from the Command? In front of him is a stage where five people sit anxiously, inspecting him with their eyes. A middle-aged woman sits in the center of the five in a larger red chair. She is the first to speak directly to Jeremiah.

"You may take a seat." She directs to him while motioning her hand towards the chair in the middle of the room. Trish shoves Jeremiah forward and forces him into the seat, facing five people on a stage who he assumes are the Appointed. The woman in the middle who directed Jeremiah to sit raises her left hand, which silences murmurs in the room like magic, but he judges it quickly as a sense of authority. He's felt magic before and won't ever forget how the fogginess tasted. How it smelled.

"What is your name?" She addresses Jeremiah. Everyone is quiet with tension, awaiting his response.

"What is YOUR name?" Jeremiah retaliates back. This causes whispers to start again throughout the crowds and even an aggressive laugh from behind him.

The woman raises her right eyebrow and smiles at Jeremiah. Her smile isn't welcoming but amused by his response; pleased with the challenge. She begins writing something down and showing it to a weasel looking man to her left. The woman has white hair that is tied tightly at the top of her head, with a large black feather wrapped around it. She and the rest of the men and women on the stage are wearing the same brown coloured robes with a blue Crystal Star emblem sewn onto them. It differs from the Varthian emblem as the Crystal Star sits in solitude without swords crossing behind it.

The weasel man to Charlotte's left has a thin string of facial hair that travels from the bottom of his lip to his strong chin. His face is skinny and sunken in like a skeleton. Beside this man is a younger woman with grey hair who is vigorously writing on paper, recording the conversations. She hasn't looked up once since Jeremiah sat down in the trial room.

"My name is Charlotte of the Varthian Fringe people and YOU are our captive. A Tradey spy," the woman says matter-of-factly, creating truths from assumptions. Her steel blue eyes are unwavering from Jeremiah's, studying him very carefully. To the right of Charlotte is a large man with bushy, red, uncombed hair and a large beard to match. He strokes his facial hair with one hand while the other is crossed over his large belly, all while looking Jeremiah up and down. Body language that suggests distrust of the boy. The fifth and final of the Appointed is a young man with blonde hair, and a brand on his chest peeking out from his robe. He is leaning in his chair with his legs apart, comfortable in his surroundings. He chews on a small piece of jerky, maneuvering it around his mouth with his tongue.

Jeremiah speaks, responding to his charges. "Charlotte of the Fringe, I hate to disappoint you and the people who've gathered here"—he gestures towards the audience with shackled hands— "but you've wasted your time. I am not a spy, but merely a slave," Jeremiah states in a calm tone. He decides it is better to be a slave at this point than a spy.

Charlotte responds almost immediately, "I'll play your game, slave. If you are a Varthian captive as you claim, then how did you get through the Fringe and onto the beach? Isn't it forbidden for *you people*?" Her voice alters almost mockingly, but otherwise her tone stays calm. She's not the type of woman who loses control and not someone you can catch off-guard.

The way she says 'you people' makes Jeremiah's blood boil. How could it be his fault that the Command has been in control of his life since he was a child. He wasn't born into freedom in the Fringe or raised as a Varthian commander. She is waiting for his response, which could alter his fate, whatever that may be. Jeremiah spots Cornelius sliding into a chair in the stands right behind Charlotte. He mouths the word 'truth' and points to his heart. Jeremiah stands up slowly and lifts his arms to the crowd to show his wrists are clear of the Crystal Star brand. He hopes that this will eliminate the notion that he is some type of Tradey spy as all Tradies have this emblem.

"I was aboard a Tradey ship, but not as a worker. I am a child transport, age seventeen and one half. The lack of a Tradey brand should have been the first indication."

The claim makes the crowd angry. "Liar!" someone shouts from Jeremiah's left. The shouting is a catalyst for more uproar from other Fringe people around the arena. He slowly reaches into his pocket, feeling for the security knife. It's a difficult task in chains, but he finds the wooden handle and holds it securely in his hand, still hidden from sight.

The weasel looking man whispers into Charlotte's ear and she nods slightly. The people around Jeremiah begin throwing rotting food and spitting at him as their rage grows, but it doesn't seem to faze the Appointed as they discuss amongst themselves. Trish comes from behind Jeremiah and strikes him across the face with a closed fist, the sucker punch of a coward. The Appointed don't move to stop her, still unfazed with their surroundings that grow more and more chaotic by the second. The unexpected blow takes Jeremiah's breath away. Trish raises her hands up to the crowd, circling Jeremiah like a boxer who's showing off with a lesser opponent. The mob cheers Trish on, asking for more. "Hit him again!" a woman yells in a shrill voice. Trish abides with a right hook, making Jeremiah's vision blurry. A ringing begins to block out the mob's shouts. He can only see out of the inside corner of his right eye and tastes blood in his mouth, spitting it onto the dirt floor in the direction of his assailant. His hand holds the knife tightly and he prepares to dodge the next hit and stab Trish. She begins punching the air while walking towards Jeremiah, gearing to strike him again. Charlotte stands up, lifting her left hand in preparation to speak, inadvertently halting the beating and mob-like yelling. Trish drops her fists in defeat, although she wouldn't say it, and walks back behind Jeremiah, smiling playfully as she passes him. Jeremiah spits blood again onto the ground in front of him. Charlotte of the Fringe people stands up and speaks loudly, addressing the crowd.

"It is our judgment that this," — she waves her hand in Jeremiah's direction, not certain what to call him — "this man shall be sentenced to —" The door behind Jeremiah bursts open, cutting Charlotte off. A figure is running towards him. The outside sunlight pours in from the open door, making it hard to see who has interrupted.

"What are you doing in here? I told you to wait at home!" Charlotte scolds the newcomer. Jeremiah turns to the door and squints his eyes, using his hands as a blockade for the blinding sunlight. The door closes, and Jeremiah sees who is approaching.

"Quinn?" He means to shout, but merely whispers under his breath. She runs directly past him and straight to the Appointed. Bowing to them partially out of respect, but also because she is catching her breath. She must have run here.

"I must humbly request that you release this boy at once," Quinn says demandingly through heavy breaths, lifting her head to make eye contact with the Appointed. Charlotte opens her mouth in response but is cut off.

"Under what circumstances?" the weasel man responds. Charlotte gives him an unpleasant look, but the man doesn't take his eyes off Quinn.

"Appointed, this boy is Jeremiah, the one who saved me and other children from the transport ship. He is a hero, not some spy." Quinn's voice has wavered from demanding to angry. Jeremiah's head hangs in exhaustion. It takes everything in him to stay awake and not pass out from Trish's blows.

"It is too late for that; we have made our decision," Charlotte responds, waving her hand in dismissal at Quinn.

"Have you issued your decree?" Quinn asks, with no response. "Well, have you?" Quinn demands again. Charlotte stares at Quinn, disapproving of her actions

49

but out of ways to challenge her. "My people…" Quinn now addresses the crowd, "I will be unchaining this boy and taking him out of this trial. He does not belong in this chair and he does not belong in this chamber. The decree has not been issued. He saved my life and does not deserve to be treated like a Tradey. I will ask the Appointed to vote on his sentence, can I get a yea?"

The crowd begins agreeing with Quinn, some yelling, "Here, here," others supporting with a, "Yeah," and some by simply clapping or stomping their feet. How quickly their tune changed in mere moments. Clearly, she has supporters in the community. Quinn then looks up at the Appointed, demanding a vote. The woman who was vigorously writing simply raises her hand without looking up from her paper. This must be one of the most interesting sessions she's recorded, Jeremiah thinks and then smiles at how caught off-guard Charlotte is. The type of woman who does not get caught off-guard often.

"Jacob?" Quinn addresses the weasel man to Charlotte's left. He smiles at her and raises his hand as a yea. Jeremiah sees that he is missing a few teeth.

"Bingley?" Quinn skips Charlotte completely. Her arms folded into her chest makes her vote obvious. The red-bearded man nods his head and stands up. He must be ten feet tall, Jeremiah judges. The man waves his hand in dismissal towards Jeremiah.

"Take him away, Quinn." She doesn't have to address the young man at the end, but his arms are folded just like Charlotte's, leaving his answer obvious.

"Well, daughter, you may take your hero and leave. This trial is dismissed, and the prisoner is released." Charlotte gets up and leaves the room before anyone else can ingest how quickly Jeremiah went from being a prisoner to a hero. The room gets loud with whispers and the people begin filing out of the chamber through side doors.

Quinn turns from the Appointed and hurries towards Jeremiah. She kneels to hold his head in her hands, assessing the damage from Trish.

"I'm so sorry," she says to Jeremiah. Not an apology of fault, but an apology of circumstance. He smiles at her through bloody teeth. Although he can barely see through his swollen eye socket, he can make out Trish hurrying past them. He raises his locked hands towards her, indicating that she holds the keys to his freedom.

"Trish, wait up!" Quinn yells to her. Trish rolls her eyes, gets the keys from her pocket and drops them on the ground by the door before leaving the chamber. At least a dozen people kick the keys as they walk out. Cornelius rushes through the doorway, shouldering Trish as he walks by. He grabs the keys from the ground and unlocks the chains around Jeremiah's wrists. They are rusty, but with a little force, they release him. Jeremiah rubs the red rings that have formed on his wrists. Quinn and Cornelius help him to a standing position and begin walking towards the door.

"Let's get him to my examination room, Quinn," Cornelius instructs. They lift Jeremiah by his arms and help him out of the trial room. He's eager to feel the warm sun and the fresh ocean breeze of freedom once again.

Chapter 7

Days pass as Jeremiah works to recover from his injuries and become accustomed to the Fringe lifestyle. Cornelius mended the damage Trish caused with his special drink that works miracles on Jeremiah's beaten in face and twisted ankle from the shipwreck. Quinn stopped by once to walk Jeremiah through the catacombs of people and tunnels. Handfuls of them smile in their direction, but the majority mumble and curse under their breath. Jeremiah is obviously not welcome, but he doesn't care, and Quinn doesn't seem to mind. She assures him that given time, they would bore of hating him. He is assigned a sleeping room with essentials like a small cot and bookshelf with candles and medical supplies, but no actual books. He sleeps most of the time except when Cornelius stops by with food and more Rekelp to assist in the healing process.

On what he thought to be the fifth day, he awoke to no pain in his head or ankle, but also no Cornelius in his room. He could tell it was later in the day. Using a side table, he gets up and knocks a piece of parchment paper onto the ground. The paper has scribbles, arrows and poorly drawn images to help him find his way around the catacombs. It was left on his bedside table with a note saying:

'Follow the map to my location. Sincerely, Cornelius.'

Jeremiah slides on a clean black shirt and a pair of tan trousers that he'd been wearing all week. The Fringe people, as he came to call the community here, share a supply of clothes that get washed once a week. Jeremiah must share Cornelius's rations until the week flips on day seven. He was able to find a leather belt to tie up the pants that are almost hanging off his body. A hand-held mirror shows that Jeremiah's facial hair is still growing long and free. If the Tradey's managed to keep their ship afloat, Varthian officials would have shaved his head and beard for the slave trade by now. The new look took a bit of getting used to, but he likes the way it makes him look older. Jeremiah runs a comb through his hair and hurries into the hallway filled with crowds of people. He pushes past the hustle and bustle of the morning with the map in his hands. Jeremiah turns the map sideways and upside down with each turn he makes. Left, then straight then right and then straight through a corridor. He does his best to coordinate around the packed halls, trying not to run into people. People of all ages, of all skin tones and of all sizes. Some of them are giant like the red headed man of the Appointed. There are even tiny people, child size, but with aged faces of adults. Inevitably, he collides with an incomer. Directly into the weasel faced man from the Appointed. The man's arms were full of papers that scatter across the ground in a fury along with Jeremiah's map.

"You should be more careful where you step, boy," the weasel man grumpily scolds him while picking up his papers and cursing people for stepping on them.

"I'm just trying to find Cornelius. Do you know where he might be?"

The weasel man huffs and sighs while picking up the papers. His hands dramatically expressing his frustration. "Bah, he's in his study, re-reading the same books no doubt. The man is insane, I tell you. Absolutely off his rocker." He stacks his papers and snatches up Jeremiah's map in the process.

"You see? He can't even draw a proper map. This is garbage. Absolute garbage." He crumples the paper in his hand and tosses it into a trash bin that devours the map.

"I'll explain the entire place to you, but I do not have a lot of time to waste, so listen closely." His hands guide Jeremiah to the side of the hallway where they are out of the collision course of people. His thick rimmed glasses sit on the tip of his long, skinny nose.

"Each tunnel has a number, you see. They are marked at the beginning middle and end of the halls." Jeremiah listens to the man but can't help being distracted when he sees Quinn through the mass of people, walking away from them. She always stands out from everyone, a lighthouse in the ocean of people.

"Are you listening, boy!?" the man asks with frustration in his voice. Mucky yellow eyes add to his weasel appearance along with small, bony fingers poking Jeremiah's chest.

"Sorry, yes I'm listening." He watches Quinn disappear around a corner.

"As I was saying, the odd numbers run North and South and the even numbers run East and West. The start, being the coliseum where your trial was held, number zero. Staircases are located at the corner of 8 and 9 and next to the coliseum. With each level you walk down, four in total, you will be at a negative number. Cornelius's study is located at the corner of 1 negative, or one level down, at tunnel 3 and 4." The man talks so fast that it takes Jeremiah a moment to retain the grid system explanation. He longs for the map Cornelius drew.

"I say, do you always come off as a dim-wit or is it just during our encounters?" What little patience the man has is wearing thin. He brushes a long strand of dark grey hair behind his ear. The rest of it is tied back into a ponytail that touches the nape of his neck. He glares at Jeremiah with wild eyes. Only when the man is still can you see a slight, but consistent shake that takes over his whole body.

Jeremiah grabs hold of his intelligence. He doesn't have many friends or even acquaintances in the Fringe and needs to win at least one of the Appointed over. "My apologies for coming off as incompetent, sir. Your systematic explanation of the catacomb grid system will exponentially assist in my daily doings. I will forever be indebted to you... um..."

"It's Jacob and you can cut the sarcasm with me, Jeremiah." The weasel man tries to hold back a smile. Obviously amused by him, but more importantly, he used his name. Everyone else calls him "boy" or spits the word "hero" in his direction with an intentional malice in an otherwise complimentary word.

Jeremiah is holding a stack of Jacob's papers in his hands. He starts scanning them and realizes they are agricultural specs, drawings making up horticultural experiments. Something stirs in Jeremiah's stomach that he isn't used to. An anticipation for what will happen next, but not the anxiety that usually comes with such anticipation. He is happily anticipating what will come... he is excited.

"Why are you smiling like that? It's just a bunch of plants." Jacob snatches the papers from his hands and begins putting them into a specific order only he would know.

"I studied at Knoen. I worked in the fields and apprenticed under the Ascetics while they were performing very similar tests to what I just saw in those papers." He swallows hard.

"Lying is unbecoming." Jacob is untrusting of the boy and begins raising his voice. "You were a slave to the Command. How could you possibly have lived on Knoen and studied with the Ascetics? Never in my life have I heard such a fib. Never in my life." He shakes his head at Jeremiah in disbelief, but also giving him a chance to answer the accusations.

"I'll prove it. Tell me how to get to you and I'll come by tomorrow to assist." Jeremiah challenges back, grabbing one of Jacob's pencils to write down the coordinates on a blank piece of paper he found amongst the pile that was dropped.

Jacob stands for a moment, looking the boy up and down with fire in his eyes. "You certainly have my curiosity. If you can make it to me tomorrow, you may try to prove your worth. For now, you've taken up too much of my time. Go see the old loon today and I'll see you bright and early tomorrow morning under the coliseum at negative 4 and tunnel 0 and 0. Is that understood?" He rests a hand on Jeremiah's shoulder and gazes into his eyes.

"Yes, I look forward to it!" Jeremiah gleams at the opportunity and reaches his hand out to shake Jacob's hand, but is left with no returned gesture.

Jacob turns back into the crowd of people that have dwindled down to almost no one. He shakes and grumbles down the hall before disappearing around a corner. Jeremiah chuckles at the eccentricity of Jacob. He looks to the middle of the hall and notes the black 2 on the wall. He now recognizes the hall as being the walk he took to the coliseum. He walks towards the staircase beside where he had his trial and finds it no problem. The stairs are dug into the stone and dirt ground. It must have taken them years to dig down four whole levels. Jeremiah gets turned around a few times, walking into a classroom of kids accidentally before one of the child size adults that was teaching hurries him out. With a twenty-minute delay, he finally reaches level negative 1 and begins walking to the corner of 3 and 4, where Cornelius' study should be. The hallways are silent now, almost eerily so. The community must be scattered to their respective jobs, leaving Jeremiah wandering on his own. He rounds onto hallway 3 when a woman appears from the opposite end along with two escorts. It doesn't take Jeremiah long to realize its Charlotte with Trish and the young Appointed man, robe wide open to display his bare chest and brand. A squinting Charlotte registers who is wandering the halls.

"Zachary, continue to the coliseum and we will see you there." Charlotte tells the young Appointed man when she recognizes Jeremiah. Zachary's muscles bulge underneath his well detailed tattoo. Black ink shaped like two birds turned away from each other create a gruesome crown atop a naked woman with long hair, covering her genitalia. Her eyes filled in black with sorrow and her mouth appears to be sewn shut.

"Mother, I'm sure Bingley will be fine if I stay behind." The man directs his words to Charlotte but has his eyes locked on the boy and Jeremiah has them locked right back. A predator sizing him up as enemy or prey.

"I will only be a moment and we wouldn't want to keep the giant waiting." She refers to the red-haired Appointed who towers higher than anyone Jeremiah has ever seen. Zachary walks to Jeremiah and shoulders him while passing.

"Nice meeting you, Zach, too bad you couldn't stay and play," Jeremiah calls to the man, challenging him. Zachary stops in his steps for a moment, registering the remark. He runs a hand through white hair matching Charlotte's colour exactly. Although the lightness is like his sister, there is a hue of warmth in Quinn's that distinguishes her from them.

"Zachary, I will not ask you again. Go. Meet. Bingley," Charlotte commands her son. Her tone dialed in on calm yet demanding with a hint of harshness. Her son continues through the tunnel and makes a sharp left down hallway 2.

"Now, what business do you have wandering the halls alone? I've been informed by Jacob that you refused to be in his service for tomorrow. That simply will not do. You will work all day, every day for Jacob in the caves at negative 4, tunnel 0 and 0. Is that clear?" Charlotte once again orders Jeremiah around. Why would Jacob tell her that Jeremiah refused to help? He decided it best to accept her orders for the time being and ask Jacob about it in the morning.

"Clear as mud. When do I get a day off?" Jeremiah always had self-time or a self-day on Knoen, surely there would be one in the Fringe. He felt a need drilled into his bones to spend every second he could with Quinn.

Charlotte nods to Trish and she walks towards Jeremiah and punches him in the stomach. Jeremiah makes a gasping noise as all the air leaves his lungs, sending him to his knees. Charlotte bends down at the waist to speak in Jeremiah's ear. "You will work from sunup to sundown in my area until I say stop. I am the leader here, hero, and you will obey me. As long as I am in command, you will be miserable, you will want to leave, but I won't let you and, most importantly, you will stay clear of my daughter." Jeremiah takes deep breaths to refill his lungs with air. He manages a nod, which suits Charlotte just fine. She grins at him slyly, horridly pleased with herself.

"One more should do it, Trish. Hurry it up," Charlotte commands her bodyguard like a dog before walking past a kneeling Jeremiah. Her shoes click down the hallway authoritatively.

Trish walks towards Jeremiah and prepares to kick his side. Jeremiah reacts quickly by grabbing her foot and pulling her to the ground. He climbs on top of her and swings a left fist to her cheek. Cornelius comes rushing out and pulls Jeremiah off a bleeding Trish before he can get a second punch in.

"Red is a good color on you," Jeremiah says while smiling.

"You are lucky the old man is here. You will pay for this," Trish threatens with a sneering smile through bloody teeth. Cornelius takes a piece of fabric from his pocket and reaches to hand it to Trish, but the gesture is batted away.

"Get away from me, old man!" she hisses at Cornelius and disappears around the same corner Charlotte did moments earlier.

"Yeah, you better run," Jeremiah shouts after her. Cornelius takes his glasses off and rubs the bridge of his nose where little marks from the rim once sat.

"I got her good, did you see that?" Jeremiah sneers. Cornelius breathes hot air onto his spectacles and rubs them clean with the cloth he offered to Trish moments earlier. He remains silent, contemplating what to say next.

"Hello? Cornelius, did you see her?" Jeremiah looks for support from the elderly man. Cornelius places his cleaned glasses onto his wrinkled face.

"Would you have stopped?" Cornelius asks the boy.

Jeremiah scrunches his face in confusion. "What do you mean?" he asks while holding his hands up to further show his confusion.

"In my day, it was common to pick up a job in your community while studying in Varthia's university. Most students took to working at the Command, but I took another route. I was a fighter." Cornelius rubs his hands together and closes his aged eyes while reminiscing. Only men born into Varthian Command get to study at the university. Cornelius must have been someone important before he came here.

"I can still remember the musty smell in the cold, underground ring. I fought men twice my size and never lost a challenge. I researched my opponents, studied them and noted their weaknesses. I had each fight planned out before it happened and knew how far I was going to take each fight. I knew my limit and how much I needed to harm the other person in order to win the fight. I knew and planned when to stop." Cornelius opens his eyes to look at the boy. "I could have taken them faster and easier, Jeremiah. The point is that I didn't. I chose not to risk their own livelihood as we were all pawns to the big players, the gamblers, the rich and the powerful. If there was a fighter who started with a jab, I'd dodge their shot, knock them off-balance and hold them in a lock until they tapped the floor to admit defeat. I fought efficiently with little harm to my opponents." Cornelius stops talking and locks eyes with Jeremiah. "It's important, when facing an opponent, to understand their job in the big picture. Is Trish the real enemy? If she is and the only way to beat her is through a scrap to the death, then I will escort you directly to her. However, if you are the man that I think you are, then we both know who the real enemy is here, and you are going to need bigger muscle to beat it." Cornelius points to the boy's head. Jeremiah simply nods his head in agreement. "Now, is that your blood or hers?" Cornelius asks while grabbing the boy's hands. The adrenaline has worn off and Jeremiah looks down at the stinging sores on his knuckles.

They walk into Cornelius's dimly lit study. The familiar smell of burning candles and old books fills Jeremiah's senses, giving him vivid memories of Knoen and Anuva. There are three bookshelves filled with old books. Everything from practicing medicine to theory books and even some that Jeremiah didn't recognize. After Cornelius wrapped his bloody knuckles, Jeremiah began looking through the collection. Cornelius sat in a chair in the middle of the room, writing on parchment paper.

"What do you know of Jacob?" Jeremiah asks Cornelius. The man stops writing and peers up at the boy from above his glasses.

"Why do you ask? Has he done something?" Cornelius asks with concern in his voice, expecting and assuming a problem. It's a reaction Jeremiah anticipated given Jacob's opinion of Cornelius.

"He wants me to work with him tomorrow and Charlotte has given consent," Jeremiah replies, not revealing what Charlotte said.

Cornelius smiles at him. "My boy, I am surprised he invited you down there. His preference has always been to work alone, and we are all in agreement. He isn't exactly a people person, but he is extremely intelligent. I am pleasantly surprised."

Jeremiah is happy with this response. "Good, I will go, then."

The rest of the day is spent reading and discussing the books in Cornelius's study. There are some that Jeremiah read and scripted at Knoen and some that are new to Jeremiah. When the great waters rose, a lot of books were scattered across the lands, which is why Knoen is so important to the world. It's the largest collection of history books in the seas. Cornelius has a vast knowledge on books which is surprising to the boy. Or would have been until he recently found out that Cornelius studied at the Varthian university, who get all their books from Knoen. One book called The Bible is of particular interest to him. Before the floods, people read, studied and discussed the same book for centuries according to Cornelius. Even Cornelius believes in the all-powerful God that the book spoke of, but he said he abandoned our world long ago, before the flood waters came. Cornelius believes that this God swallowed all his followers into the skies and let a darkness have control of our world. Jeremiah thought Knoen contained all the history books known to existence, but Cornelius reminded him that the Command put the Librae there and filled it with the books. Could it be possible that they exempted some of the old books in order to alter history to be what they wanted? It's a lot for Jeremiah to think on and eventually, they walk back to his room.

Jeremiah finds clean clothes, some sort of porridge and a note near his bed from Quinn.

Hi Jer!

I haven't seen you around in a couple of days. I will stop by tomorrow around lunch time. Hope you had a good day.

Where Charlotte brings darkness, Quinn brings light. She is the hope, the small candle and the good of the community. If Charlotte has a child punished for stepping on her dress, Quinn is there to wipe its tears and soothe its pain.

"Quinn is a sweet girl, isn't she?" Cornelius comments, causing Jeremiah's whole body to jump. He'd forgotten the old man followed him into his room. Jeremiah simply smiles at Cornelius and nods his head in agreement.

"Well, I better get back to my room now. I'll excuse our lessons from tomorrow. I can see you will have a full schedule. Make sure you are back here for dinner time." Cornelius closes the door softly behind him.

Jeremiah eats two spoonsful of the porridge before lying down, exhausted from the day. He thinks of the one Cornelius calls God and how he sent his son down to remove his people from the lands before letting darkness fill the world, and the oceans to rise and consume masses of land. Why would the Command not have these books scripted and studied in Knoen?

Jeremiah believed they held all books there, but what if they hid some. What if some books were too powerful to leave in the hands of the Ascetics? It doesn't take long for Jeremiah to drift to sleep, questioning all he thought he knew.

Chapter 8

Jeremiah wakes up and grabs the new black shirt Quinn left for him the night before. He pulls it to his nose and takes a deep breath in. It smells like a fresh ocean breeze with a hint of lavender and mint. He slides the shirt over his head and then pulls the tan pants up to his waist. The new clothes fit much better than what Cornelius was giving to him. Quinn picked his sizes perfectly. Cornelius had been to his room moments before and gave him a hardboiled egg and some bread for breakfast. He wasn't to meet up with the boy until dinner time but wanted to wish him well before his day with Jacob. Jeremiah barely chews his food before racing out the door, anxious and excited for his day. For his purpose.

The hallway is once again filled with the Fringe people, all hurrying to their daily assignments. Jeremiah left the map Cornelius gave him yesterday, feeling confident that he can navigate the tunnels without a guide. He reaches the stairway next to the coliseum and begins walking down the levels. The first level is for meal prep, cooking, sleeping quarters and offices for the Appointed. The second level down is where the clothes get made, sewn, cleaned and distributed along with some more sleeping quarters. The third level is where things get made like bowls, beds, lanterns, tables and other types of living things. It's also where Cornelius's office and medical rooms are. By the time Jeremiah gets to the fourth level down, he is the only one left on the stairway which is visibly not as beaten down with traffic as the other sets of stairs. The end of the stairs leads to hall zero which goes under the coliseum, the opposite direction to the rest of the living areas. He walks down the dusty path that winds for an awfully long time. It's eerily quiet and only lit by an occasional torch on the side of the walls. It's little help in the darkness of the underground tunnels. After a few more minutes of walking into the dark, he approaches what appears to be the end of the tunnel. There is a large black door with torches on either side and a golden knob. Jeremiah wraps his hand around the handle and tries to open the door, but it doesn't turn. He knocks on the door, hoping that Jacob will be inside. There is no answer. Did he come all this way for nothing? He decides to knock once more and even calls out, "Jacob, it's Jeremiah. The door seems to be locked." He pulls on the knob and door once more and it opens. A little girl with a dirty nose and wearing a grey dress is on the other side. She smiles widely at Jeremiah and grabs his hand to guide him past the entrance.

"Woah," Jeremiah whispers under his breath as he takes in his new surroundings. A giant circular cave with an open roof, reaches to touch the sun that glares down on them. He judges the walls of the cavern reach upwards two hundred meters with a large bottleneck opening creating natural lighting that fills the cave. A small creek enters through the back wall. Someone has manipulated nature with the stream, forcing it into the ten greenhouses sitting in the middle of the cave and back out another hole in the rocky wall. Birds flying overhead look like little flying ants from inside the cave. He imagines the seagulls thinking the same of him. Jacob appears out of one of the greenhouses and looks over at Jeremiah who is still holding the little girl's hand. She lets go of him and races over to Jacob, hands outstretched to greet him. Long grass covers the entire cave floor, creating a natural carpet. Her bare feet kick up dirt as she jumps into Jacob's arms. He tucks her chin-length black hair behind her ear and uses his sleeve to wipe the dirt off her nose. He then whispers into her ear and sends her off to play.

"You made it." Jacob smiles at Jeremiah and extends his hand to greet him. It's a welcoming approach compared to their encounter the day before.

"Yes, thanks to your explanation on the grid system." Jeremiah half jumps to meet Jacob's hand.

"Well, let's get right to it." Jacob leads him into the different greenhouses. There is a slight arrogance in the weasel man's voice as he shows off his work to Jeremiah. The greenhouses are filled with herbs, fruits and vegetables that look extremely healthy. To say Jacob has a green thumb would be an understatement. He single-handedly started the green cave, as he calls it, and routed the stream into the rock wall and through the greenhouses to allow for easy caretaking.

"How many people are underground?" Jeremiah asks, surveying the food Jacob has grown.

"Too many, I'm afraid. We cannot continue to support the population underground. We had another cave, but it's been taken up by dastardly chickens and goats." Jacob rubs his wrinkled brow. "Despite my efforts to inform Charlotte, she continually dismisses me, saying it will get taken care of. Whatever that means."

The little girl watches Jeremiah closely as he gets the grand tour from Jacob. He tries smiling and waving at her, but he gets no pleasantry returned. She just watches him, studying him with her big yellow eyes. Jacob continues talking about how they snuck into Varthia years ago and raided their stash of seeds to start the green cave. At the final greenhouse, Jeremiah sees that there are some flowers and not vegetables.

"This is Lily's greenhouse," Jacob explains as the little girl comes in and grabs Jeremiah's hand. She leads him to the flowers. Jeremiah kneels to her level, pushes his nose into a red rose and breathes in deeply. "Smells good," he compliments her. She mimics his smelling and nods back to him before running out of the greenhouse.

"Lily is my granddaughter," Jacob tells Jeremiah in a solemn voice.

"Where are her parents?" Jeremiah asks while picking dead heads off a daisy bush.

"They are long passed now. Casualties of the Command, I'm afraid." He clears his throat and the emotions with it. "Our Lily here is lucky to be alive." He pats the little girl on the head, and she smiles widely at him.

"It's a slow day today and I think Lily and I can take it from here. Would you mind coming back tomorrow? I would like to erect another greenhouse and frankly can't deal with the Fringe people. Their complete incompetence nearly cost us the entire potato crop last season." Jacob grumbles back into his normal self.

Jeremiah is still stuck on Lily and her parents. Quinn said she would meet him around lunch time, and it must be getting close now.

"I can meet you tomorrow. Same time, same place?" he asks. Jacob simply nods at the boy and leaves the greenhouse. There is something he isn't telling Jeremiah, but he decides not to push any more. He sticks his tongue out at the little girl and gets a squished face back from her before leaving their sanctuary. Everyone must also be out during lunch hour as the halls are buzzing with the Fringe people once again. He races up the four flights of stairs and arrives at the hall to his room. He sees Quinn standing there, looking through the mob of people for something. Jeremiah waves his hand to get her attention and succeeds. Her searching gaze lands on him and she smiles with satisfaction, finding what she was looking for. She races through the crowd and jumps into his embrace. He releases what seems like the breath he's been holding since he first arrived at the Fringe.

"Are you ready for our escapade?" she asks, glowing in excitement.

"I was born ready for an adventure with you," he replies with utter assurance.

Chapter 9

Quinn sits in her bedroom, brushing out the dreadlocks that formed in the year she had spent outside of the fringe. She takes an oil that smells like coconut and runs it through her dreadlocks while brushing softly, careful not to completely ruin her hair. It's been matted before and a younger Quinn had simply cut it all off. She has more patience now. The first time she left home, she was only ten-years-old. Hearing of kings and queens in Varthia ruling as a wealthy city with more resources than what was in the Fringe was intriguing to a ten-year-old Quinn. Charlotte's absentee parenting combined with no father in sight made it easy for her to leave. She longed to see more than underground catacombs. While her mother was busy pushing mandates with the Appointed, Quinn trekked through the Fringe only to get caught by a Varthian patrol and thrown into the slave trade. Mud-covered, skin and bones, Quinn chose to not speak when she was caught and it protected the Fringe community. She led the Tradies to believe she was mute and was sold to a Varthian chicken farm on Jopwen. The only other child transport was a 12-year-old Jeremiah.

Quinn shakes her now half-dreaded hair with the tips of her fingers, rubbing dreadlocks away and gazing at her reflection in a wooden framed mirror. She smiles, thinking of a young Jeremiah who was just as broken as she was.

"Quinn, what are you doing with yourself today?" Charlotte stands in the doorway of her daughter's room, looking at her with arms folded.

"Nice to see you too, Charlotte." Quinn doesn't turn and face her mother. They stand in silence for a moment until Charlotte takes the brush from Quinn and starts working through her daughter's matted hair.

"Why do you insist on leaving the Fringe? This is the third time you've left this place only to come back months later looking like a Spryte flower-child. It doesn't reflect well on your brother and I." Charlotte brushes harder, pulling more hair than necessary.

"Status is always your first concern, isn't it? I've been back for almost a week and this is the first time you've come to see me. I can't stand this place you've created. It seems as soon as we aren't worried about merely surviving, greed sets in like a plague. Greed of materials, greed of comfort and greed of power." Quinn looks at her mother in the mirror's reflection knowing that last point would hit home.

Charlotte meets her daughter's eyes. Quinn triggered the reaction she knew she would. "My, what a horrible life you've led. If your father were still here I'm sure he'd be so proud of his little runaway."

More silence fills the room as words are left unspoken.

"So, where were you this time, Quinn? Running with chickens in Jopwen? Staying a kilometer away and stealing supplies to sustain you? You really think that counts as being resourceful?" Charlotte recounts the last two times Quinn left the Fringe, the same ammunition loaded and fired, over and over again. She's put the brush down now and picks up a doll made from straw and fabric sitting on Quinn's nightstand.

"I followed the man who was here before. The one in the cloak that you met just outside our borders. Was he wearing a Varthian uniform?" Quinn admits fearlessly.

"You should watch your step, Quinn. I'd hate for you to disappear again. My daughter, the runaway." Charlotte threatens, placing the doll into her daughter's hands and walking out of her room.

Quinn feels her whole body relax with Charlotte's energy leaving the room, releasing the tension that was being held. When Quinn's father was killed by the Command on a resource mission to Varthia, Charlotte was never the same. Instead of a human being and a mother, Charlotte turned into a cause, a determined force to abolish the Command and Varthia. Quinn's brother, Zachary, was old enough to remember their father. Perhaps that's why he was swayed into the same cause. Quinn, on the other hand, was a free spirit. She didn't have a cause or a belief, but she knew right from wrong like the difference of black and white, guided by humanitarian ethics instead of a cause with no moral compass.

Quinn left the fringe three times in total. The first time was when she went to Jopwen for a year. When she returned, Charlotte shed a tear at the sight of her lost daughter found. It was the only time she truly hugged Quinn. The second time, Quinn left when she heard her mother and Trish scheming about placing a bomb in the Varthian slums. Despite Quinn's pleas to Charlotte to not hurt innocent people, Charlotte was determined to cause chaos in the capital of the Command. Quinn took the equipment, sabotaging her mother's plans and stayed just outside the borders of the Fringe. Cornelius checked up on Quinn frequently and encouraged her to stay away from the Fringe until her mother calmed down. It was not uncommon for Charlotte to remove obstacles blocking her cause, in whatever means necessary.

The last time Quinn left, she really did follow Charlotte. Though she never found out who the visitor was, she suspected her mother had a hand in her capture. She only spent a few weeks on a fishing island called Carr. Quinn knew if she proved herself useless, they'd ship her back to Varthia.

Quinn never found out what her mother was doing meeting with Varthian uniformed strangers. She guessed Charlotte wanted power, more power than the Fringe had to offer. Quinn suspected that Charlotte has always been in contact with Varthia and that eventually there would be an infiltration. One can only live in catacombs underground for so long before the other side starts becoming appealing. At least, that's what Quinn and a few others in the Fringe suspected.

With her dreadlocks brushed out, Quinn sets out to find Jeremiah to escape from the catacombs for a little while. To forget the vile woman who gave her life. To avoid Charlotte and the cause.

"The forest between Varthia and the beach is constantly changing. The trees move their branches, the paths change from sand to moss and the leaves change colors whenever they please," Quinn explains to Jeremiah as she guides him through the forest, grazing the soft bushes with her right hand as she walks. She speaks of the land like it's a living, breathing being. Her hair has been combed out and hangs in hundreds of small braids. She wears a purple flower in her hair and a fitted brown dress that shows off her small figure. Jeremiah is entranced by how gracefully she maneuvers under fallen trees and over boulders. She leads with confidence and grace, even with the ever-changing path.

"Why didn't you tell me you came from here?" Jeremiah asks Quinn. They spent a lot of time together on the Tradey ships, telling each other secrets and stories. Not once did she mention her home.

"We made a pact to make up our backstories, remember? It was your idea! I liked being the warrior princess of Ma'ar." Quinn turns around coyly with emerald eyes smiling at him. He shakes his head and smiles back. She doesn't look young to him any more as she grabs a piece of green fruit from a tree and tosses it to Jeremiah. He watches her peel the fuzzy skin off and eat the pink inside. A drip of the juice escapes down her chin and onto her neck, rolling along her ivory skin and down her chest. Of course, he remembers convincing her to make up their history. It was easier than facing the abandonment, beatings and chaos within his own. He peels off the skin of his own to expose the fruit inside, mimicking her technique.

"How have your people hidden this long from the Command?" he asks Quinn between bites. It's a question he silently asks often but hasn't had an opportunity to voice.

"Are you kidding? The Command won't step foot in this forest. We've only had one intruder since I was born, and he ended up staying with us. The Command has no clue we are here."

A tree branch moves to the right and changes its leaves from maple brown to white flowers. "Whoa," Jeremiah whispers in awe of the transformation.

"Or at least, are too afraid to travel inside." She laughs at the thought of Varthian soldiers being afraid of a forest.

"Charlotte says a Spryte colony lives in these woods. I believe the forest changes to protect us. We respect the forest, unlike the people of Varthia. This is an ancient forest and Sprytes don't like when the Command cuts down their friends... the trees." Quinn turns to Jeremiah and is met with a very confused expression. "You don't know what a Spryte is, do you?" Jeremiah shakes his head, no. Quinn smiles at him "It doesn't matter, they are make-believe anyways. My mother Charlotte used to put me to sleep telling me stories like that." She stumbles through what to call Charlotte as the term mother doesn't feel right.

Quinn makes a sharp left behind a boulder and stops moving. Jeremiah bends over trying to catch his breath. This is the most exercise he's gotten for a long time. Between being held captive on the Tradey transport and healing from his beating, courtesy of Trish, he's out of shape. He looks up and is faced with a wall of pale green foliage. Quinn slides her hand into Jeremiah's and guides him through the wall. It seemed dense from the outside, but in the blink of an eye, they are underneath the biggest willow trees Jeremiah has ever seen. Their long, thick leaves guard an oasis underneath them like a canopy. Deep purple and sunset orange flowers speckle the long, soft grass. An ice blue pond sits directly in the middle of two giant trees. The sounds of the forest are almost eerily silenced in here, but in a peaceful way. Quinn points to a deer at the water that doesn't look the least bit alarmed by their entry. She looks up at them, but with curiosity and not fear. She finishes her drink and walks slowly towards them, stopping not even a foot from where they stand. Her head is almost at the same height as Jeremiah's. She stands for a while, sniffing the air in front of them before going back through the wall of foliage. Jeremiah reaches out to touch the deer as it passes, but Quinn grabs his arm, shaking her head.

"We must not touch, only look. We don't want to compromise our relationship with her." Quinn walks into the middle of the willows and takes a seat by the water. She motions for Jeremiah to sit with her. Jeremiah watches as she scoops water into her hands and drinks. He makes his hands into a cup like hers and scoops water into his mouth. The liquid is perfect with a cool temperature and sweetness to it that Jeremiah can't compare to any other taste. He feels refreshed from one scoop but wants more. He bends over to scoop more, but Quinn stops him.

"Only take what you need, don't be greedy, Jer." He feels out of place with all these rules but trusts Quinn, especially in this place. It feels old, like many have lived and died within.

Almost as though the trees have stories, secrets. The knowledge of what was, is and can be.

"Did the others survive from the ship?" Jeremiah asks Quinn. It's the first he's thought of Keedo, Sydney and Scotty since he was washed ashore. Quinn stares down at her reflection in the water and begins playing with her hair. Her once happy smile turns into a frown.

"Sydney had too much water in her lungs, I couldn't save her. She was dead before we reached the shore. Keedo and Scotty were taken by the Command, but I was able escape into the forest. Charlotte wouldn't let me send a rescue team. No exceptions, especially outsiders." Quinn's eyes begin to well up with tears. Jeremiah watches one stream down her face. He's not seen this sensitive side of Quinn before. Even on the Tradey ship, she didn't shed a single tear. He raises his hand to console Quinn by rubbing her back but stops just before touching her. She wipes the tears from her eyes and stands up. Her head tilts straight back to look up at the canopy of willows. Above them, the sun plays peek-a-boo through the thick branches and long leaves. Quinn reaches for Jeremiah's hand to stand him up and he seizes it welcomingly. She wraps her hands around Jeremiah's waist and he softly places his own on her lower back.

If feels like a million tiny butterflies are inside his stomach, trying to escape. He never wants to leave Quinn's side. He could stay forever in this moment.

A snapping branch near the willow wall snaps them out of their embrace. Trish barges in through the wall. "Foolish, girl! You shouldn't bring strangers here. I'm going to have to report you to the Appointed," Trish shouts.

"He's not a stranger and go ahead, tell my mother. I'm sure you will be praised, and she will adopt you so you will live happily ever after together," Quinn retaliates in a sarcastic tone, clearly looking to taunt her. This makes Trish's eyes widen in anger and bolt towards them. Jeremiah grabs Quinn's hand and they race around the pond, away from Trish and back through the foliage wall.

"Get back here!" Trish yells as she gets smacked by a moving branch that seemed to almost hit her intentionally, like it was protecting them. Jeremiah looks to ask Quinn if they should stop, but she is too busy laughing and running back towards the catacombs. Her laugh is contagious, and Jeremiah can't help but join in her bliss. He helps her jump over a fallen tree, they hop on rocks across a stream that formed since they were in the willow trees and stop in a clearing with blue glass in the center. Quinn collapses on the grass in the clearing, laughing and smiling. Jeremiah is bent over catching his breath, admiring her happiness. He's never met someone so carefree, so in love with life.

He reaches his hand out to help Quinn up from the soft grass. She walks over to the blue glass globe in the middle of the clearing. As Jeremiah walks over, he remembers the ceiling in the courtroom. This is what it looks like from the outside. They wander over and investigate the room. It is empty now and looks like an inconspicuous cave from up here.

"We really should get going," Quinn says as she looks up at the sun as if it were a clock, telling her the time. "Tonight, is our Crystal Jubilee. Cornelius will be able to help you get ready, go and find him and I'll meet you at the celebration." She leans in and kisses his cheek before prancing away into the forest.

He brushes his cheek where her lips were once planted before realizing he doesn't know where to go. "How do I get back into the underground?" Jeremiah yells to her, but she is already out of earshot. He looks around at the forest, entranced by how peaceful it is here. He begins to understand why Quinn wouldn't tell him about this place before. It's a secret even he would keep from outsiders. He walks over to the court room and tries to remember how big it was, retracing his steps back through the door and to the right where the cavern would be. Sure enough, through a tight lineup of trees, he is looking down the side of the catacombs with their skeleton filled tombs. He grabs a vine leading down the side and rappels himself to the ground with ease. His leg muscles ache from his adventure with Quinn. Jeremiah follows the cavern through the quick turns and is once again at his quarters. Cornelius is sitting on a rocking chair, reading what looks to be an old reference guide like a dictionary or encyclopedia. Old eyes look up from over round glasses and a frown forms on the man's wrinkly lips. His hair has been combed and he is wearing ironed pants with a burgundy dress shirt.

"You are absolutely soiled. Never mind now, we must get you bathed for the evening festivities. You need to begin adjusting to this culture or Charlotte will never fully accept you here." Cornelius grabs Jeremiah's arm before he can protest, leading him to a room across the hall where a bath awaits. Jeremiah can't remember the last time he had a bath. Cornelius points to a pile of clothes on a bench.

"Put those on and I'll leave someone to escort you to the hall," he tells Jeremiah before closing the door behind him. Once again, Jeremiah is left with questions in his mouth and no one to answer them. The bath is filled with scalding hot water. He begins thinking of his time with Quinn in the forest. Why was Trish so angry with him being under the willows? It seemed like a sacred place to both of them. The way the water tasted, the sweet-smelling air and the canopy of willow trees; it was surreal to Jeremiah. He gets out of the bath and begins putting on the clothes that Cornelius set out. He slides on the beige cotton pants and fits his head through a blue t-shirt that has three buttons on the top which he leaves undone. There is another piece of clothing with two holes that Jeremiah struggles with a couple times before discovering it's for his torso. He uses a sharp pair of scissors to clean up the thick forest that's formed on his cheeks and chin. A hand-held mirror reveals a face that Jeremiah doesn't recognize. He feels like a new man. A sudden knock at the door makes Jeremiah jump. He opens the door and is greeted by the Appointed man with the red hair. He looks much bigger now that he is standing up; three times the size of a regular man.

"Well, well, well don't we clean up nicely?" the man says to Jeremiah with a chuckle, looking him up and down while stroking his red beard. "Give us a spin, sir, so I can get a look at ya." He reaches to Jeremiah's shoulder and pushes him in a circular motion. Jeremiah is caught off-guard by the man's forward disposition and loses his balance from the strength of his shove. The man stops Jeremiah from falling over with both watermelon sized hands on the boy's shoulders. "Oh, where did I leave me manners? Bingley Toppet is the name." He introduced himself with a graceful bow and a flick of the wrist.

"I'm Jeremiah." He smiles at the giant's mannerisms, completely disregarding any normal social etiquette or personal space. Bingley's red cheeks and sparkling blue eyes are filled with a contagious warmth and excitement.

"Ha! I know who y'ar! Well, enough jabbering, let's get to the hoo-ha, huh?" Bingley says while motioning towards the hallway.

Jeremiah nods at Bingley and begins walking down the corridor and onto the Crystal Jubilee.

Chapter 10

Large wooden doors swing open by two lightly armored guards, revealing a giant dining hall. At least twenty large tables are filled with boar, roasts, potatoes and other dishes that Jeremiah doesn't recognize. He closes his eyes and takes a deep breath through his nose, capturing the intoxicating aroma. There is a stage-like structure at the back of the room where a group of men and women bang on drums and strum string instruments, creating music. Some of the little people form a circle and perform synchronized dancing while spilling drinks they hold carelessly in their childlike hands. Children play tag in between their parents and fellow Fringe people. A boy steals a kiss from a girl in the corner, making her cry instantly and he laugh in playful bliss. People are running, dancing and shouting throughout the room, caught up in the festivities. It seems like complete chaos to Jeremiah, and he loves every second of it. For once, he feels a sense of belonging amongst Quinn's people.

"Bingley get over here, ya big brute!" a man with the same build and accent as Jeremiah's escort shouts. Bingley gets a hop in his step towards the man, bursting into a hearty laughter that shakes the candle chandelier above. He gives the man a big hug, almost lifting him off the ground and sits at the table with many men and women of the same large stocky shape as Bingley. Each one of them shouts and laughs with no apologies for their boisterousness. Jeremiah realizes he has been left alone with no invitation to join Bingley's group. Panic sets in as he looks around and doesn't recognize anyone. He has been alone all his life. Why now does he feel unsettled without company? Where is Quinn, where is Cornelius? He can feel his heart beat faster and feels suddenly hot. It seems like everyone is looking, pointing, whispering and laughing at him — the stranger, the spy, the outcast. Five, four, three, two… he closes his eyes and begins counting down in his head to calm his heart.

"You can't expect to experience our culture with your eyes closed, hero." Charlotte speaks just above a whisper. The word hero slipped off her tongue in disdain. The hairs on the back of his neck stand on end. He turns around and opens his mouth to speak, but Charlotte raises her hand in his face as if to silence him. Jeremiah reaches up and slaps her hand — it was something his best friend in Jopwen used to do. The place after Knoen.

"It's called a high-five," Jeremiah says to a stunned Charlotte and gives her a wink. The boldness irritates her, but her cold gaze does not alter from his facetiousness. If anything, she's grown to expect it. Her hair is pulled back tightly again, and her pale skin shows no sign of aging apart from a scar above her right eye, small but deeply wrinkled. A black flower holds tightly to her hair, one that must have been manipulated black as it's not a colour of nature. The Crystal Star shines at Jeremiah as a pin that stands out on her worn red dress. New clothes must be hard for them to come across. He wonders the significance of the Crystal Star to the Fringe people. It's a sign of Varthia, the culture and the people. Curious that they share a symbol of reform in a freeing place like the Fringe. The irony is fitting for Charlotte.

"I'm not sure your intentions here, but my daughter will not be one of your pawns." The harsh woman interrupts Jeremiah's thoughts. "Your influence on her will end immediately. You made it through your trial, but you will not last much longer here, I can assure you." She smiles and laughs at a joke neither of them tells as if covering up her threats from onlookers. He reaches up and touches her shoulder, smiles and walks away without another word. Charlotte nervously rubs her hand across her head, smoothing out any hairs that may have come undone.

Jeremiah starts walking around the room, ingesting the encounter with Charlotte. Trish must have told her about their meeting at the sacred willows. The Fringe people stare and whisper as he walks around the great hall. He sees some type of orange liquid on a buffet table and pours himself a glass. He chugs the liquid and pours himself a second. It has a sweet flavor, but the aftertaste is bitter. He coughs and shakes his head, trying to get the taste out of his mouth. A group of girls around his age walk past Jeremiah, whispering and giggling to each other. Scanning the room, he still can't find Cornelius or Quinn. The music stops and a horn sound causes the crowd to migrate to the stage. Jeremiah follows the crowd but gets stuck at the side of the stage with a poor view of what may be happening. Charlotte takes center stage and raises her silencer hand to instantly quiet the crowd.

"Welcome everyone to our Crystal Jubilee Commemoration. As we celebrate 100 years of solitude in our underground sanctuary, we must also remember the losses that made it possible. Let us take a moment of silence for the brave men and women that sacrificed their lives for our freedom." Charlotte bows her head, rests her right hand over her pin which would be sitting on top of her heart, if she had one. Jeremiah noticed everyone else was doing the same. He took the moment to scan the room for familiar faces. Where could Quinn have gone? He feels a sudden tug on his shirt and looks down to a little girl with disapproval all over her small face and eyes. Jeremiah quickly bows his head and whispers, sorry, to the girl with a side smile. Charlotte wipes an imaginary tear from her face with a square piece of cloth and continues her speech.

"Now, as we continue our evening, please remember to be responsible with the liquor, respectful to your fellow Fringe people and safe on your route home. Let's give a round of applause for the lovely music headed by my son, Zachary," Charlotte says while openhandedly pointing to him.

"One more thing before I surrender my time on stage, there will be a special surprise for everyone at exactly ten p.m. Please do not retire until this time. Fringe be the victors!" She ends her speech and the rest of the congregation repeat the same phrase back in a unified, "Fringe be the victors!" Finally, her speech is done, and she exits stage left. Jeremiah looks down at the little girl again and bends down to speak to her.

"How do you tell the time all the way down here?" Jeremiah asks the little girl.

She points to a large structure on the right wall that Jeremiah now recognizes as a clock from his studies at Knoen. He scratches his head trying to remember how they work and judges it's eight-thirty p.m. He smiles at the girl, pats her on the head and starts walking away. Jeremiah sees a ladder that must have been used to hang the decorative linens on the ceilings. He makes his way through the crowd and climbs the ladder to see if he can scout out Cornelius or Quinn. He scans from the front doors to the stage and back again but can't see either of them. When his eyes scan to the stage for the second time, he sees Charlotte behind scraps of old sails on the stage that make up curtains. She is fidgeting with her hair and dress while tapping her foot anxiously. Trish jumps onto the stage instead of using the stairs and walks behind the curtains to Charlotte. She whispers something into Charlotte's ear. Charlotte looks to be scolding her for something and points for her to leave again. Jeremiah follows Trish with his eyes. He sees her walk over to a buffet table and scoop herself some of the orange drink. She is wearing a purple and black long dress, but Jeremiah can see her combat boots and pants underneath. She tugs at the dress in an uncomfortable fashion, a fish out of water with such an elegant gown on an unrefined woman. Jeremiah looks back at Charlotte who is still behind the curtain, but now there is a hooded figure with her. They have moved further behind the curtain and in the shadows. Jeremiah wouldn't be able to see either of them if he had been on the ground. In fact, he must be the only one in the room who can see them. The figure is taller than Charlotte, and Jeremiah judges it is a man from his hairy arms and broad shoulders. They continue speaking to each other and Jeremiah notices something on the man's left wrist. It's the Tradey symbol! His stomach drops to the ground below. What kind of man is Charlotte meeting with in the shadows? The symbol on the left wrist is Varthia's way of marking the worst kind of criminal.

"Jeremiah! There you are!" Jeremiah hears Cornelius calling to him from below. Charlotte's neck cranks to where Cornelius is looking, and the hooded man backs into the darkness behind the stage. Charlotte calls for Jacob in an attempt to summon him, but he ignores her with a shake of his hand in the air and continues talking to a group of Fringe people.

"Jeremiah, come down from there!" Cornelius shouts again. Jeremiah looks down at Cornelius whose looks and tone suggest something is wrong. Jeremiah almost slips, quickly trying to descend the ladder. Bingley must have recognized Cornelius's tone as he walks towards them.

"Something is wrong. I can't find Quinn," Cornelius says to Bingley and Jeremiah.

"Why would you assume something is wrong? Maybe she is just late," Jeremiah suggests as he takes a final step off the ladder.

"Bingley!" Cornelius turns to the giant. "Charlotte keeps brushing me off and saying, 'she will get here when she gets here'. Something is wrong," Cornelius pleads to Bingley for belief.

"Aye, yer might be onta somethin'. How 'bout the boy and I go looking for 'er?" Bingley suggests while placing his hand on Cornelius's shoulder.

"Yes, I'll distract the guard at the south entrance so you can escape and find her. Do hurry, I've got a sinking feeling this surprise may not be good." Cornelius turns in a flash and starts into the orange liquid. One cup, two cups then a third.

That must be the liquor Charlotte was talking about earlier. He takes his glasses off and tucks them into a pocket on his shirt.

"Bingley, I don't understand, why would Charlotte be behind Quinn missing?" Jeremiah asks.

"Charlotte's been thirstin' for power since she got appointed. Quinn has been spyin' on her to try and find her out." He rubs his big hands together anxiously.

"She was with a man earlier. I saw them speaking and he had the Tradey mark on his left wrist." Jeremiah marks the crossing of swords with his finger on his left wrist.

Cornelius is talking to a younger looking man guarding a single door to the right of the stage. He begins to stumble a bit — acting out the effects of the liquor. The guard takes Cornelius to sit down at one of the tables a few feet away from the door.

"We have to move quickly, boy, put some spit in yer step." His large hand motions for Jeremiah to follow him. They successfully sneak out without being caught. The doorway leads them to a dimly lit hallway.

"Which way, now?" Jeremiah asks.

"I haven't the faintest," Bingley responds looking back and forth down the empty hallway.

Chapter 11

Jeremiah closes his eyes and concentrates on the sounds in the underground hallway. Bingley's breaths are heavy in and out. A hole in the ceiling lets in a steady 'drip, drip, drip' of water from above. The tiny feet of a mouse scurry up a wall to his left. Then it happens. A new sound reaches Jeremiah's ears from further down the hallway — footsteps that are getting louder and louder as they approach. He grabs Bingley's shirt to guide him into the doorframe. The newcomer's footsteps round a corner down the east wing, coming straight towards them. Jeremiah holds his hand up to Bingley, telling him to be quiet. The person races past in a flash, but they got enough of a glimpse to know who the newcomer is: Trish. They sneak behind her, hiding in doorways and corners along the way, following her and making darkness their ally. She winds through the maze-like tunnels, left then right, two more lefts and into the trial room. The Varthian Star above lets in almost as much light as the sun. They hide behind the entrance door, watching her lift a rug underneath where the Appointed sit. She reaches down and pulls on a latch attached to a door and quickly disappears into the ground.

"Where does that lead?" Jeremiah asks Bingley.

"I'm not sure. We always enter from the front room." Bingley rushes to the door in the ground. He counts down ten seconds with his sausage-like fingers before opening it. A set of brightly lit concrete stairs invite them to carefully climb down. Bingley shuts the wooden latch door softly and more importantly, quietly. The last thing they want is Trish to notice them following her. Small flames held by cobweb covered wooden handles line the walls, dimly lighting the way down about forty steps. When they get to the bottom of the stairs, they reach a perfectly square room with no sign of Trish anywhere. Jeremiah hears a low and steady 'thump... thump... thump' that he passes off as his heartbeat. No other sounds indicate where Trish could have gone. They've reached a dead end.

Bingley bends down to the dusty ground, examining where dirt has been disturbed. Two footprints lead to the far wall, but their owner is nowhere to be seen. There are engravings on the tunnel wall. Jeremiah's hand wipes over the dust, revealing over a dozen stick figure drawings, each with two or three figurines. He examines the engravings closer and realizes each set is being killed or injured in some way. One is being thrown off a cliff into a chasm of doom, another is being stabbed with a spear and one more is strapped to a wall with knives being thrown at it. He brushes his hand over the last one. Its face is expressionless, but it creates a burning inside Jeremiah as he remembers the Tradey's doing this to him.

The boy hits the drawing with a closed fist. "Where did she go, Bingley?"

"Mine's as good as yer guess, boy. She's vanished inta the thin of da'air." Bingley looks up at the boy from his crouched position. Both hands scratch his combed back hair until it's back to a messy state, back to normal. Jeremiah likes him better this way. Clean cut doesn't suit him. The giant takes a big breath in through his nose and sighs loudly while standing back up, defeated.

The steady 'thump, thump, thump' in Jeremiah's head is driving him mad. He pounds his fist into the wall again just above Trish's vanishing footprints. "Dammit, Bingley, we need to find her." A loud creak and rumble comes from the wall, opening a hidden passageway to more stairs.

"My boy, I think ye found the way!" Bingley swats Jeremiah on the back in a victorious manner. "We must tread with lightness fer da path may not be safe. Follow me slowly but lead a backward with haste should ya sense trouble amidst." It takes a moment for Jeremiah to understand the giant's warning, but follows him into the darkness regardless, trusting his companion.

The winding stairs through the dark opening seem to get steeper and steeper as they lead further into the darkness. Spiderwebs line the walls and holes in the earth, which indicate this area of the tunnels isn't well maintained. They get one hundred steps down with no sign of the staircase ending and are left in complete darkness when the hidden door slams shut. The steps begin varying in size and cause Bingley to slip backwards. Jeremiah grabs the giant man, but is little help given his size. They slide down the steps, helplessly falling until they hit a landing.

"Y'all right, kid?" Bingley asks Jeremiah while brushing his hair out of his face. It sticks to his sweaty brow, a magnet to metal. Luckily the giant acted as a cushion for Jeremiah, both uninjured from their fall.

A flame to their right shows them a corridor. Another flame, flickers light further yet, indicating movement in the distance. "Trish…" Jeremiah whispers and quickly helps Bingley up to continue their pursuit. They walk through the corridor, using the darkness to conceal them should she be watching her back. Another female voice echoes at the end of the hall.

"Help! Help me please!" Quinn's sobs echo off the walls but are quickly overtaken by Trish's blood curdling laughter.

"Heeelp, heeelp me pa-pa-please," the woman mocks her captive.

"You're a monster," Quinn shouts back, not defeated yet.

"Me? A monster? Oh, princess, if you only understood. This whole thing is much bigger than you could possibly imagine, and we can't have you ruining everything. Nor can we have you screaming any more." Trish strikes Quinn across her face with a strap of leather wrapped around her fist. Jeremiah's jaw stings at the sight of the beating. He knows Trish's blow all too well. Water covers the ground around a helpless Quinn, strapped to a chair with a mixture of blood, bruises and tears running down her cheeks.

"Ruin what? What is Charlotte doing?" Quinn demands.

The steady 'thump, thump, thump' gets louder. Trish points her hands up in the air and a realization punches Jeremiah in the chest — she can hear it, too. A sinister grin overtakes her face and Quinn's assailant begins cackling and jumping around while singing with the beat.

"The drumming comes at night,

and it brings him such delight,

He will land upon the silver shore,

and we will bow to call him lord!"

At this, Bingley gets up and runs straight at Trish. "Ye devil woman! How dare ye call him 'ere. Ya think he will stop at your enemies? He would gladly scrape your insides clean and feed it to the sea." He tackles Trish to the ground. What little efforts she makes to escape the giant's iron grip are futile. He soon has her arms tied with the same leather straps she was using to beat Quinn. Jeremiah runs to his friend and uses the knife Cornelius gave him to cut Quinn's straps. He opens his arms to hug her, but she side-steps his sentiment and darts towards Trish, punching her in one fluid motion. Trish only laughs harder and spits blood in Quinn's direction.

"I told you, Bingley, I told you and Cornelius that's what she was going to do!" A mixture of blood and spit spray from her words. A passionate 'I told you so'. "Charlotte's an evil woman who thirsts for power that's no more quenching than sea water."

"Aye, Quinn, we realized too late. We must get ye outta 'ere before they come." Bingley drags a now screaming Trish to the chair that was once Quinn's prison.

"You can't be serious?" Jeremiah pipes in. "He's coming, and he will kill everything. Ever wondered why there are no survivors? You can't hide, you can't run — we are all walking dead." Jeremiah's hands clench in a fear-filled anger.

Quinn rests her hand on his shoulder. "We have to at least try, Jer."

The boy nods his head in agreement, but his heart knows better. His studies at Knoen were thorough and no one in all the history books had survived an attack by Lord Demetrius. The only stories are of the disaster and death he leaves. Bingley finishes tying up Trish and walks back through the hallway to the stairs, assuming the others would follow.

"You can't leave me here!" Trish screams in a terror-filled demand. "I will find you, hero, and I will rip out every limb of her body in front of you! I will pluck every hair out of her precious head and force her to choke on her own tongue while you watch. I will get my revenge if it's the last thing I do."

Quinn turns away and grabs Jeremiah's hand to follow her. He lets go and doesn't move. A statue frozen by hatred. This woman who has caused so much pain dares to threaten them. His legs cemented; captivated by her anger. She continues yelling threats into the air and tries with all her might to release herself from the restraints, moaning and shouting.

"Lord Demetrius's men would love some Quinn company, I'm sure of it. Every last one of them will have his turn with her!" She spits one last threat with a cold red grin and locks eyes with Jeremiah. A disturbed look takes over her face, contorted in fear and her once frustrated scream turns horrific.

"It's Him! He's here!" Blood streams out of her eyes and nose as she points her boney finger directly at Jeremiah who hasn't strayed his gaze or moved a muscle. Blackness has slowly crept into his eyes, filling them completely. The 'thump, thump, thump' gets louder and faster now.

Bingley runs back into the room, alerted by Trish's screams. He tries to shake Jeremiah out of his trance. The boy simply raises his hand and swats the giant to the ground like a fly.

"Quinn, what's wrong with him?" Bingley cries out as the drumming gets louder and louder.

Quinn slips her hand into Jeremiah's, instantly awakening him. The drumming slows to a heartbeat intensity. Jeremiah breathes deeply and looks at Quinn and Bingley curiously. "Why are we still standing here, we have to go!" Bingley motions to Quinn to not speak of what happened as the boy clearly doesn't remember.

"You two head up, I'll be right behind yas. Hurry now." Bingley's oversized hands push Quinn and Jeremiah out of the room. Once they are out of sight, the giant walks slowly to a pale Trish. Her body is slumped over on the chair with clear liquid oozing from her mouth and nose. He rubs the liquid coming from her mouth and touches it to his tongue — salt like the ocean. Her once brown eyes now filled with blackness. He pushes her eyelids closed and backs out of the room superstitiously, leaving Trish in her tomb.

The trio make their way up the winding staircase with a flame Quinn grabbed off the stone wall. Ten steps from the top, the doors open, and they slip through without any struggle.

There are screams coming from down the hallway followed by a blood curdling roar that stops them in their steps. The attack has started.

Chapter 12

"We must get yus out of 'ere." Bingley hurries them. "There's an exit to the top down the hall, but we must pass the main corridor." The three of them waste no time and hurry through a roofless cavern where Jeremiah is thankful to smell the ocean breeze.

The full moon eerily peeks through thin clouds but looks like a dim light next to the brightness of the Varthian star, bluer than Jeremiah had seen before, like it's watching over them. Quinn runs ahead, allowing Jeremiah to see the back of her left ankle had been slit, bleeding at each step she takes.

Admirable strength, when mere moments ago she was being tortured. He starts wondering what happened to Trish. There's a blackness surrounding his memory between her bellowing threats and them walking up the stairs from the torture chamber. Why can't he remember what happened? They round a corner to face a figure standing in front of them, slightly hidden in the shadows. Each breath the figure takes creates a rumble through the corridor, shaking the floor and walls. The figure is taller than Bingley, but fitter, and carries a sword in his right hand that reflects the full moon. He lets out a fierce noise that could be described as a roar, but not mighty like a lion. This growl creates a pain in their chest and a ringing in their ears that brings Bingley, Quinn and Jeremiah to their knees. It's a growl that shakes the ground, straight from the depths of the earth. The figure reaches his arms to the ground like a gorilla, and charges towards them with the sword in his mouth. Bingley makes a poor attempt to stop the creature but is quickly swatted to the side with little effort by their attacker. Its gaze directed at Jeremiah remains unfazed by a giant and a girl. Quinn lies in the fetal position, holding her ears with her hands, moaning in pain. The smell coming off its cold skin reminds Jeremiah of a Tradey — old liquor, salt water and toxic waste. It holds up its human-like, grey colored hand with black, long fingernails and pushes Jeremiah's hair back to gaze into his eyes.

"Get away from me, devil!" he yells and spits in the creature's face but it doesn't flinch, unfazed determination. It takes the sword from its mouth and pushes it to the side. 'Why isn't it killing me?' Jer wonders. It sniffs him and then lifts its head back and starts howling. Suddenly a sword swings, cutting the howl off as it slices its way through the creature's grey neck, and a boot sends the head across the room while the lifeless body collapses onto Jeremiah. Black oozing blood races onto his stomach, but he feels an incredible sense of relief. Cornelius shoves the creature's body off Jeremiah and helps him up.

"Boy, am I happy to see you." A relieved Jeremiah accepts the old man's help. He runs to Quinn and helps her up from the ground where she was still paralyzed from fear and pain of Lord Demetrius's creature.

"We need to get out of here, now." Cornelius continues down the corridor and towards the exit. They round the final corner to their escape. A wooden spooled ladder leads to an opening above. Cornelius pushes past them. "I'll take a look outside to make sure it's safe." He climbs the twenty spools to the top and looks all around, checking for any creatures. "It looks clear, Jer, why don't you have Quinn —" Before he can finish, another creature jumps down, grabbing Cornelius on the way. Bingley picks up a nearby boulder and smashes the creature's head into the ground repeatedly, in a futile attempt to save the old man. Blood spills from Cornelius's neck and he begins convulsing as the creature's black blood runs into his revealed flesh. His eyes roll into the back of his head. In between short breaths, he whispers something that makes Jeremiah lean in close to translate the old man's dying words.

"...kill me." Cornelius's grey hairs fall out of his head and his wrinkly skin turns grey like leather. His legs and arms break and crack as they become larger and thicker — turning into a creature. Quinn screams in terror at Cornelius's transformation. Bingley cups a hand over her mouth and hugs her head into his shoulder, speaking to the girl in a tongue Jeremiah doesn't recognize. Jeremiah slides his hand in his

105

pocket and grabs the knife Cornelius gave to him before his trial.

"Goodbye, my friend," Jeremiah whispers into Cornelius's ear as the old man's irises change to jet black. He opens his mouth to scream, but instead the creature's growl escapes his mouth and his body violently thrashes. Jeremiah saws Cornelius's neck with the blade until his screams stop and his head detaches from his body. Quinn and Bingley stand in shock.

"Let's get the hell out of here," Jeremiah huffs while cleaning his blade on scraps of Cornelius's ripped clothing. There's no time for mourning their loss. They climb the ladder to find themselves in a clearing.

"The coast is this way; I have a boat there." Quinn leads the others. They walk through the forest which seems to be mourning with them. The trees move their branches with every step the group take, and the dirt lights up a faint blue color, creating an easy route to the coast. His friends are silent, in shock. Questions circle Jeremiah's mind. Why had Charlotte called Lord Demetrius to their sanctuary? Why were they able to escape? He breathes in deeply and exhales, trying to bring calm to his heart and mind. The way the cool breeze hits Jeremiah's nose, reminds him of his second home on Jopwen.

Chapter 13

An eerie fog sets in on the town of Jopwen. The hot summer days always end in cool nights, bringing a thick fog into the streets. The small town's square was always buzzing with people in the daytime. Governed by the Varthian Command, its market is one of the most commonly used ports for goods and services. At night, it's silent. At night, the ships are docked and Tradeys fall fast asleep at the inns. Not this night. This night, an almost seventeen-year-old Jeremiah is battling an older boy under a lamppost in the cobblestone streets. Jeremiah climbs a tailor shop's steps with a sword in hand. He pivots his foot and jumps at the boy, clanging his sword down onto him.

"Not bad, for a milkmaid," Jeremiah berates the boy who is built heavy but trained to only half of Jeremiah's sword-skills. The boy's amateur stance makes him easy to get off-balance.

"Easy, Jer, I don't know as much as you," the boy begs to Jeremiah, but his pleas are ignored. As a Gladius Domini's assistant, Jeremiah spends his entire day assisting his Master Gregor with swordsmanship. Renowned as one of the best swordsmen in the seas, Gregor received prestigious visitors. People sailed from all over to throw treasure, goods and other offerings at him for training, but he wouldn't accept bribes. Gregor trained who he wanted, when he wanted; a man of honor and of wisdom but lacking any sense of reserve. He was a harsh master, one with the kind of ego that forces a boy to find comfort in the freedom of the night. The empty cobblestone alleys of this sleeping island were Jeremiah's playground.

"Mercy will teach you nothing," Jeremiah shouts to the boy, a phrase he hears Gregor speak almost every training session. Jeremiah constantly waited on the man, greeting him with tea in the morning, a cloth to wipe off sweat during trainings, an overcoat should he step outside for tobacco, and parchment if he needed to send out a letter. Although he never got training himself, he remembers and practices everything from watching his master at work.

Jeremiah charges at the boy, coming in from the right, stepping to the left to avoid an off-balance strike, ducks, spins and strikes the boy in the side. The boy falls to the ground and a determined Jeremiah lifts his sword in the air and brings it down hard as if to finish the boy off. He is stopped halfway to his victim's throat by the sight of blood on his sword. A soft light from the lamppost glistens off the crimson drips coming from Jeremiah's weapon. The boy's eyes well up with tears and he moans in pain, holding his side. Jeremiah drops his sword with a clang as it hits the cobblestone ground and echoes through the empty streets. He reaches to help but is shoved away as the boy disappears in the blackness of an unlit alley, fleeing his attacker and whimpering the whole way out of sight. A black puff of air leaves Jeremiah's mouth as he breathes out, like he was smoking an unfiltered cigar. He had gone too far again, a bloodlust he didn't comprehend. Looking left and right, he makes sure no one witnessed his accidental attack. The sword lies on the ground and, for a moment, Jeremiah doesn't pick it up. He entertains the idea of leaving it for someone else to find. For someone else to get carried away and slice the dairy farmer's fat son open. He grabs it anyways and darts in the opposite direction of the boy, climbing a staircase to the butcher's roof. He jumps from ridge to gable, balancing on the roof peaks and ducking past hanging laundry. The sun ever so gently rises over the east wall, creating a blood red canvas on the sky. Jeremiah hops over the back wall of Gregor's palace and makes a long jump to an open window, barely catching it with the tips of his fingers. He lifts himself into the opening with trained confidence that only comes with practice. He hides his sword in the floorboards of the kitchen and climbs into his makeshift bed in a closet. With eyes closed, he thinks of the boy he sliced open. Why didn't he stop? Why couldn't he be more careful? It seemed like a dream to him; like his head was filled with a dark fog and he couldn't stop himself.

He drifts into an in-between where he is back fighting the boy. This time, they are atop a cliff in the clouds, and fully armed from head to toe in Varthian uniform. The boy has that terrified, uneasiness in his eyes as Jeremiah charges towards him. He steps to the left and slices Jeremiah's arm open. The gash shines red but isn't deep enough to cause heavy bleeding. Jeremiah charges at the boy again from the right. He steps to the left to avoid the boy's strike, ducks, spins and strikes the boy across the side in a fluidity even Gregor would applaud.

Jeremiah's head doesn't have the fogginess from earlier. His mind is clear with one directive — he needs to kill the boy. He raises his sword and slices down like a knife through warm butter as the boy's head rolls across the cliff. A black bird comes from the sky and lands on the boy's head, picking out his eyeball for a snack. He looks up to the sky as it turns black with heavy clouds. Jeremiah closes his eyes to smell the crisp mountain air. It smells like rain. He opens his eyes as water comes down on him like a waterfall.

Back in his room, his head soaked with water while the cook, Trixy, stands over the top of him, empty wash bucket in hand.

"I tells you not to stay out all night, I tells ya a million times, but did that stops ya? Nah!" She points her dark-skinned finger in Jeremiah's face, scolding him.

"Okay, Trix, I'm awake now. What time is it?" Jeremiah groans back at her, feeling like he hadn't slept for more than a few minutes.

"It's ten minutes ta his mornin' tea, boy, and I don't feels like stitchin' you up this morn'. Gots enough on my own plate, Mr Jeremiah, with the Masta inviting that Varthian Admiral for dinna." Jeremiah pounces out of bed and grabs a new shirt. "You best hurry to the kitchen, I prepped the masta's tea for ya so you'd be on time," she tells him as she stands with her muscular hands on her curvy hips.

"Thanks, Trix, you're the best," Jeremiah tells her, kisses her cheek and heads out to the kitchen.

Trixy shakes her head and laughs as Jeremiah runs through the hallway. "Dat boy be trouble," she mumbles to herself while making his bed.

Gregor was a petite, muscular man who seemed to walk with a protruding arch in his back, shoving his chest forward and his plump behind out. His awkward stature had no disadvantage to his form, though. Jeremiah had a lot of experience with the man's back hand. The bruises help develop character, Gregor would tell a grimacing Jeremiah at least twice a week and usually with a half empty whiskey bottle in hand. Jeremiah didn't get bothered by it, though. He kept doing his work during the day and enjoyed his nights fighting on the streets and watching the sun rise over the rooftops.

Jeremiah watched Gregor train a young boy from a wealthy family. The boy was small, wimpy and uninterested in learning the art of the sword. He was quickly dismissed by Gregor walking out of the training area, yelling for Trixy to take the boy away and muttering something about unfit lineage. Jeremiah watched the small boy sit cross legged and cradle his chubby adolescent cheeks in his small hands. He felt envious of the boy. He would do anything to have opportunities that this boy was born with. The boy was privileged to have lessons with the great Gladius

Domini, Gregor. To practice sword fighting in this arena that has trained so many greats before him including Varthian Commanders. An idea struck Jeremiah as he watched the boy anxiously chew his fingernails. An idea that had the potential for grave consequences. When Gregor was fast asleep, he would sneak into the arena and practice. He was tired of the uneven cobblestone streets, beating the baker's son — he needed to know what it felt like to practice on the arena floor. To practice like a champion. Jeremiah the Gladius Domini.

That night after finishing his chores, he sneaks onto the stone floor. The moon shines a spotlight for Jeremiah, a lone actor on his stage. He takes a knee and rubs his callused palm across the floor, feeling the softness of the stone. Jeremiah always watched the trainings from the shadows. This was his first time being in the center of the arena and he never wanted to leave. He stands up and closes his eyes to bring back the memory of defeating the boy on the street. With his eyes still shut, he pivots his body, steps to the left, ducks, spins around and jabs his imaginary opponent in the side. Another win for the good guy. The small arena comes alive with imaginary applause and a trophy from a beautiful matron. The crowd cheers louder as he shows off his moves with the sword. He throws it in the air, catches and spins it around his back. Then, he mixes a few jabs and kicks with the striking motion as if he's battling multiple opponents. The crowd claps their hands together in a roar of entertained excitement. *CLAP, CLAP, CLAP*. Jeremiah turns around as real clapping breaks his imagination. Gregor is clapping his hands, but his face does not look impressed.

"Good show, slave." Gregor slicks his black hair behind his ear, takes a swig of rum and walks around a speechless Jeremiah, sizing him up. Jeremiah sees that Gregor has a steady, gloved hand on his holstered sword while the other hand swishes around the almost empty bottle of whiskey.

"Now, tell me; how did you make such a remarkable replica of a Varthian sword and how did you happen upon these skills?" Gregor asks a still speechless Jeremiah.

"Come now, slave, tell me now or I will force it out of you." Jeremiah doesn't dare respond but is fearful of fighting him. If he tells the truth, he's dead, but if he stays still, he will have to fight Gregor. How did Gregor know he was out here, anyways?

"Very well, young slave, raise your sword like a man." Gregor places his sword ahead of him in a fighting stance. Jeremiah stole the sword from a

Varthian guard when Admiral Devonshire was getting his monthly training. He purposely spilt hot water on the Admiral's guard and received a licking from Gregor in consequence but was overjoyed with his cleverness when he slipped away with the weapon. Gregor snaps his sword towards Jeremiah's face, breaking the boy's thoughts. The sharp metal slices him open near his right eyebrow, but he doesn't flinch.

He simply stares forward into the distance, hoping if he ignores the drunk, he will let him leave unharmed.

"That was your warning," Gregor says while throwing his rum bottle against a stone pillar with a crash. "You know why I only give one warning?" He questions the sixteen-year-old statue.

"Mercy teaches nothing," Jeremiah mumbles.

"Oh, so you DO pay attention to my trainings. This must be how you got those cute moves. Now, en garde!" Gregor pounces towards him, but Jeremiah instinctually bats his sword away and slices the back of Gregor's calf.

"You insolent little brat!" Gregor shouts while grabbing his leg. "I'll have you hung for this!" Lights in the house turn on and Trixy races out, placing a piece of fabric onto Gregor's wound. Gregor throws his sword onto the ground and marches inside, howling in pain.

"Mr Jeremiah, you need to leave now, ya here?" Trixy says to a stunned Jeremiah. "Did ya hear me? You need to run while ya can." Jeremiah remains still, stunned and unsure where he is to go. Trixy grabs Jeremiah's shoulders. "Run, stupid child." His feet take off, running through the iron gates of Gregor's estate and into the cobblestone streets. Where was he to go? The town was small, and Gregor would find him if he willed it and Jeremiah was confident, he wanted him dead. He purposely makes his way to the shipyard to be captured by a Tradey transport. The same Tradey transport that reunited him with Quinn. The one that shipwrecked off the coast of Varthia. The same Tradey transport that led him here.

Chapter 14

"Jeremiah, snap out of it!" Quinn snaps her fingers in front of Jeremiah's face. Bingley is looking at him with a concerned look.

"Sorry, guys, I was... uh... thinking." He shakes his head back to reality.

"Best pull over for a nap, methinks. We've put a fair distance between us and the tunnels. We have another twenty miles to Varthia's wall. The Lord did prolly put a scour on 'em coasts for any persons makin a break, anyhow," Bingley guesses while stroking his beard. "Trees should offer us the best protection," he continues while pointing to a cedar five times the width of Bingley and at least two meters to the first branch.

Quinn makes a running jump to the tree, pushes off a small knot in the middle of the trunk and barely grabs a higher branch with her fingertips. She moans in anguish but is quick to get a better grip and swings her body onto the branch. A quick three branches higher, she moves around the tree and settles close to the trunk. Magically, the tree creates a cocoon-like bed for Quinn to settle into, reinforcing just how deep her bond is with the forest.   Bingley is next; he starts by running to the tree and jumps at it like Quinn, but instead of pushing off the knot, he grabs it with both hands, pushing down with his upper body and feet and projecting himself up to the first branch. He maneuvers his way around the trees, selecting only the big branches, being conscious of his size, and settles on a double branch to hold him. The tree groans and leans to the side from Bingley's added weight and quickly another tree grows out of the ground to create a bigger cocoon bed for the giant. Next is Jeremiah who isn't the least worried about climbing the tree. He was always a good tree climber on account of his fingers' grip. It feels like glue has bonded him to the tree when he touches the trunk. There has never been a tree he couldn't climb. No matter the size, shape or type of tree, it's never been a challenge for him and his wood-glue fingers. He settles into a braided branch above Quinn. Within minutes, Bingley is snoring, open mouthed, without reservation. A lot of Bingley's disposition lacks formality or a sense of shame. It's the part Jeremiah likes most about his giant friend. Exhaustion sets in as the adrenaline leaves Jeremiah's body. The worry of Lord Demetrius's men catching up to them, or worse, one of the creatures finding them makes it hard to fall to sleep. He rests one of his hands on his chest, feeling his heartbeat at a fast pace. His other hand dangles below and is quickly held by Quinn's. The tree moves their cocoon beds closer to each other. All around them, grape vine and bushes grow high to create a barrier of safety between their sleeping tree and the rest of the forest. A defense against the dark forces crawling through the Fringe. Jeremiah counts to one hundred and twenty stars in the sky before falling fast asleep.

Chapter 15

A yellow finch lands on Jeremiah's head and sings into his ear, waking him from his rest. The sun has just begun rising, painting a crimson sky like a memorial of the blood that was shed that night. He hears whimpering coming from below him where Quinn is resting. "Quinn, are you awake?" he asks softly.

"Yes, sorry if I woke you," she apologizes as the cocoon branches open to reveal tear marks on her cheeks. Jeremiah swings himself down beside Quinn. She doesn't hesitate to rest her head on his chest. He hadn't thought about how she must be feeling. She was betrayed by her own mother and left to die in the hands of Trish. Not to mention seeing her entire home stripped away in minutes by Lord Demetrius.

"Jer, do you remember what happened to Trish?" Quinn questions hesitantly.

"Of course, I do," he snaps back. "She was… she…" Why can't he remember? He was there with her in the underground dungeon. He can still see her restrained to a chair, laughing like a mad woman, but then there is blackness until they are climbing the stairs back to the main corridor. "I can't remember." Jeremiah looks at Quinn, lost for thoughts.

"Jer, I think you killed her." Bewilderment strikes Jeremiah. "She was talking about torturing and killing us, and you were… overtaken by something."

"What do you mean I was overtaken?" Jeremiah shifts his body away from Quinn, studying her face for answers. Her once tamed hair sits matted from sleep.

"You were still there, but a darkness took over. Your eyes turned black and then she was dead." Her eyes look to the ground as she nervously plays with a golden lock of hair. "It was frightening and yet so amazing. She was pure evil, Jer, we all wanted her to die."

Memories of the Jopwen street battles drift into Jeremiah's head. It feels the same as when he sliced the boy accidentally. It feels the same as when he was a child on Knoen, releasing hurricane winds in his shack in anger of betrayal. This time is different, though. This time, he couldn't retrieve the memory of hurting Trish. How did he lose control and what took over? He needs to be able to control himself. He can't let the darkness have power. Quinn caresses his cheek and brings his face close to hers.

"You don't scare me, Jer. Not one bit." And she presses her soft lips to his. They sit in silence for a while with his arm around her back and her head on his chest. He holds her hand and gently strokes the indentations of her palm with his fingertip.

"I don't understand how we are still here, Jer. No one survives Lord Demetrius's attacks. There has to be a reason for why we are still alive." Quinn looks to Jeremiah for answers.

"It's okay, Quinn, we are safe now," Jeremiah reassures her, but he can't help wondering the same thing. No one survives an attack from the Lord. His stomach is in knots. He can't fight the feeling that there is still danger to come. They need to get off the island.

"I think we better wake the giant." He kisses her forehead and makes his way over to shake Bingley awake.

"D'ar the drinks are o'er on the table, Yark," Bingley mumbles sleepily, stuck in a deep dream.

"Come on, Bingley, we must get going." Jeremiah shakes the giant again, but he is fast asleep. The trees must have heard Jeremiah's pleas as a branch grows leaves and swats the giant on his red nose to wake him. He jolts awake, knocking Jeremiah backwards off the tree in a swift motion. Falling, he reaches to the tree, trying to grab onto anything to stop his quick decline. He closes his eyes to brace the ground's impact, but it doesn't happen.

Quinn lets out a gasp followed by a question Jeremiah will never forget. "What are you?"

His eyes open to see his left arm has merged with the tree, inside the tree and the skin around this bind has turned the same texture and colour as the large oak.

"Get me down! It's got a hold of me!" Jeremiah yells at Bingley who is now on the ground, reaching up at the boy to help.

Bingley tugs on Jeremiah, but he can't get him loose. "There's only one way ta get outta messes ya don't wanna be inta. Ya gotta member how ya got in thur first and follow the crumbs back again." Jeremiah closes his eyes. He was thinking of falling when he merged with the tree. A panicked thinking that he didn't want to fall, that his fingertips were going to catch him from the pain of hitting the ground. His eyes open, but he isn't released from the tree.

"It's not working, Bingley!" The boy touches his half tree-half skin arm with his normal hand, completely mesmerized at the transformation.

"Don't think of how you got there! Think of how to get out. Imagine being freed and having your arm back," Quinn instructs from the ground. Jeremiah nods and closes his eyes again. This time, he barely imagines himself being released from the tree before he is in freefall, again. Luckily, he has a giant friend on the ground who catches him and stands him on his feet in one fluid motion.

"Are you okay?" Quinn asks followed by, "How did you do that?" without allowing Jeremiah time to respond. He is looking his hand and arm up and down. It looks normal, but whatever that was wasn't normal.

"Like the girl from my in-between," Jeremiah whispers aloud.

"What's an in-between?" Quinn stares in awe at Jeremiah.

122

"Boy, you do have some trickies up them shortened sleeves, ahem, I reckon!" The giant grabs Jeremiah's arm to look it over. "Seems like some witch trickeries to me if I ever saws them."

"It's not trickery and I'm certainly not a witch. I don't know what it is, but I see a woman in my sleep who does this. In-between wake and sleep I have visions, and she runs through the trees," Jeremiah explains to his wide-eyed companions.

"Der's more ta' him than meets our eyeses, huh. Quinny?" Bingley bats Quinn's shoulder and roars loudly with laughter.

"Still not scared of me?" Jeremiah asks the girl in what he intended to be playful but translates his insecurities clearly. He can't hide his feelings from her.

"You're amazing," she reassures him, grabbing his hand to affirm her acceptance. The giant starts walking as the grapevine and trees, that acted as their guard, sink back into the ground. A path forms as they step, guiding them to the cove that will offer their freedom from Varthia. Jeremiah can't fight the feeling that they're battle isn't finished yet.

Chapter 16

The cove greets them after what seems like hours of walking. A beautiful purple sunset reflects off the waters like a perfect painting. Quinn collapses on the rocky beach in exhaustion, but Jeremiah barely notices. He is taking in the sights and sounds of their freedom. A small freshwater creek runs into the ocean to their left. Bingley reaches into his big coat pocket and reveals animal skin carriers that he passes around. Jeremiah sees a small fishing boat tied to a thumb shaped rock and walks toward it. He looks inside and is happy to see some stale bread, oars, a small fishing rod and an axe. There is a room below the deck with a small bed that a mouse has made his home judging by the droppings. One small but sturdy sail sticks up like a beacon on the boat. A large sunflower print blanket, a few shirts and even a pair of pants all sewn together make up the sail. Bingley carries a shuddering Quinn into the bed and drapes his coat overtop of her. Jeremiah touches his hand to her forehead and finds that she is burning hot.

"Bingley, what's wrong with her?" The giant shakes his head and ties his hair back with a piece of string.

"The shock's getting to her. She needs more rest, ma boy."

Jeremiah unties the rope holding them to shore and sets it into the boat. He stares into the forest that was once a refuge, now tainted with death and destruction. Their clear path to the cove has changed back to its grassy state and the trees have moved to hide their passageway. Bingley puts his arm around Jeremiah's shoulders and bows to the forest, bending Jeremiah at the waist to bow with him. The respect Quinn and Bingley have for this forest is endearing to Jeremiah. They both care for it like it's a living being. Though the boy doesn't quite understand it, he feels a debt of gratitude for the forest giving them safe passage. A strong wind that seems to come from the forest warms him from inside his stomach to his toes. The hairs on his neck and arms stand on end and the trees seem to moan in unison. It's the same feeling he got from the willows with Quinn. Bingley stands up and turns both he and Jeremiah to the boat, pushing it into the water and away from the island of Varthia.

"How long had you lived there, Bingley?" Jeremiah asks.

"Since I was a wee babe." The giant sighs while manipulating the sail with his back to Jeremiah. After a moment's struggle, Bingley sits again keeping his eyes forward towards the ocean, curiously ensuring his eyes don't face Varthia.

"Why haven't you looked at the island since we left?" Jeremiah asks, while staring back at the forest.

"I'd rather be facing where I'm going then thinking where I've been." This leads Bingley into a song that Jeremiah hasn't heard before.

"In the current, we be floatin

Makin' way for the settin sun

No care for where we goin

And no time for where we been.'"

The words of the song seem to carry in the wind and out to the sea.

"She be the star to guide me

She be my mornin' sun

She be there to greet me

When my life be done."

Jeremiah scans the cove, searching for signs of followers. Lord Demetrius's legend is known across the seas. He doesn't leave survivors. He must be hot on their trail, and time is frighteningly against them.

"Bingley, it feels like we've been sailing for hours, my friend. Why are we not out of sight, yet?" Jeremiah's anxiety is peaking.

"Aye, we're getting caught in the tide. This vessel be not my first choice, but once we get to the open waters, we'll move much speedier. Alls I ask is yer patience," Bingley grunts while gripping the tiller.

Jeremiah's gaze falls back to the island. A woman appears on a rock by the shore. Jeremiah can see her long black hair dancing in the wind and is reminded of the woman who visits him in his in-between. She raises her arm straight in the air, almost in salutation.

"Bingley, do we have a tele in this heap?" Jeremiah wants to see her closer.

"'Fraid not, ma boy. Quinn only kept emergency items aboard." Bingley tightens the lines to the jib, causing the boat's pace to quicken. They must be losing the pull of the tide.

Jeremiah stands up to get a better view of the woman, but she has turned and is running back into the forest. Although he can't make out her face, there is no denying that she runs into a large cedar at the edge of the trees, just like the woman from his in-between. His eyes widen at what he sees, and he pinches himself to make sure he is awake. A groggy Quinn slides beside Jeremiah and rests her head on his shoulder.

"Did you see her, Jer?" she asks through a yawn.

"See what?" Jeremiah's shirt flies behind him like a cape in the strong wind

"The Spryte. She sent us a blessing for our journey."

Jeremiah feels the temperature in the air drop and rubs Quinn's arm to keep her warm as they are carried further and further out to sea by the wind. At this moment, Jeremiah has a calm revelation; the woman in his in-between is a Spryte.

Chapter 17

The bright moon reflects off the black water in such a magical way if you happen to be at sea during the night. It's like the world doesn't end but continues from high in the sky to the depths of the ocean. Jeremiah and Quinn lie on their backs and count the stars in the sky, manning the boat while Bingley rests below deck. The wind has died down and the warmth of the world greets their skin once more. Quinn's white hair almost glows in the darkness of the night. Everything about her mesmerizes Jeremiah. Even with scraped knees, untamed hair and smudges of dirt on her cheeks, she is stunning. He watches her tell a story of the Spryte Goddess, Samara.

"She lived on Lost Soul Island, you know, before Lord Demetrius came to be. The island was once a beautiful place of exotic flowers, the tallest of trees and happy creatures. It wasn't always his lair." Quinn explains while pointing towards the sky, like she is painting a picture. "He tricked her, Jer. The full moon turned black and darkness rose. He brought death and destructions to her sanctuary. Legend says only she can defeat him, so he trapped her in a star and sent her to live in the skies alone."

Jeremiah looks to where Quinn's finger is pointing and can't help but laugh. "You mean to tell me that Varthian's Crystal Star is a Spryte and that Lord Demetrius put her there instead of killing her?"

Quinn giggles with him and playfully covers his mouth to stop his teasing laughter. "Quit laughing, I told you it's a legend. She was betrayed by him and he couldn't bring himself to kill the one thing in this world he loved. Lord Demetrius chose a path of evil power, but his love remains for Samara. Even if it's not true, you have to admit, there is something beautiful about a love so hopelessly tragic."

"I'd like to think he's just a man with a heart and a soul same as you and me. One whose tyranny and destruction are only matched by the Varthian Command. Matched and necessary enemies of these waters." Jeremiah nods in agreement with his own opinions.

"Jer, I hate to tell you this, but no one is the same as you." Quinn strokes Jeremiah's arm that had transformed earlier that day.

She isn't wrong, he thinks to himself. The darkness and rage that has taken over in his past, lost memories of hurting Trish, the woman in his in-between and his newly found "ability" rush through his mind. The memories shuffle around in his mind like an endless nightmare of unanswered questions and fear of what is to come.

Jeremiah hugs Quinn into his chest and they fall asleep to the sound of the tide lapping against their small boat.

Chapter 18

The Spryte woman greets Jeremiah in his in-between again. This time, he is standing face to face with the creature. Her blue eyes sparkle like the Crystal Star and look upon him intimately. He touches the surprisingly smooth skin on her hand and is captivated by her beauty. The setting is the same as all of his other dreams. They are in a beautiful meadow with wildflowers, and warm sun beating down on them. She holds her forefinger to her lips as if instructing him to be quiet and points to a bush, silently telling him to hide. He isn't sure how he can understand without her speaking but lies on his stomach under the bush without hesitation. She presses her full lips to his forehead, filling him with a warm sensation from the place her lips touch. She stands in plain sight and screams just like in his regular dream, but this time he will be out of sight when the shadow comes. His view is obstructed by the low hanging bush. All he can see is the blood rain at her feet. Then, two black boots appear. Her feet remain planted as the black boots come towards her. Why doesn't she run? Jeremiah thinks to himself. Suddenly she is lifted from the ground and Jeremiah can hear choking noises like she is gasping for air. The shadow is strangling her! Jeremiah can't stay hidden any longer; he gets up and charges into the blood rain. A sword magically appears in his left hand and he raises it to strike down the villain that's haunting his in-between. The shadow turns its head, stopping Jeremiah in his tracks. It is dressed as a full Varthian guard with slick black hair and a grin that Jeremiah knows all too well. The shadow is a version of himself. It throws the lifeless body of the Spryte to the ground without altering its gaze from Jeremiah. It grabs the sword from Jeremiah's hand and spears it into the boy's stomach in a fluid, determined motion.

"Your weakness is offensive," the shadow whispers into Jeremiah's ear and throws him to the ground next to the Spryte woman. It walks away into the blood rain as thunder crashes above them. Jeremiah is facing the Spryte woman once more. She seems to be smiling at him as her body slowly vanishes from the ground and is carried into the sky, taking her place as the Crystal Star. He feels pain from his stomach where the dark version of himself stabbed him. He feels cold, like he is dying in his in-between.

He jerks awake with a sleeping Quinn in his arms. The sun is just piercing the sky, waking the world from its sleep. Bingley snores loudly from below deck. Jeremiah sneaks his arm out from under Quinn without waking her and pulls Bingley's coat over her bare shoulders, tucking her in. He grabs a fishing rod and ties a squirmy pink colored worm to the hook before tossing it into the sea. He learned how to fish in the ponds of

Knoen. Jeremiah could make a rod and bait out of anything and come up with the best catch of the day. Bingley appears above deck and smiles at Jeremiah while stretching towards the sky with a big yawn. Everything is big and loud when it comes to his giant friend.

"Any luck with the fishes?" Bingley asks through the end of his yawn.

"Not a bite, yet." Jeremiah tugs at the rod to make his bait more desirable to the fish. A light wind picks up a leaf from the boat, taking it dancing through the sky and dropping it delicately on top of the light blue water. Jeremiah looks all around their boat for sign of land, or worse, a ship. There may be something in the distance, but the sun likes to play tricks on men at sea. A thick fog begins to roll in as well; making it difficult to see their surroundings.

Bingley has loaded a fishing rod with two worms and prepares to cast his line. He brings his weight onto his back-right foot, pushes off with a jump, spins around and releases the line into the sky, shaking the boat with each bounce. It's the farthest cast Jeremiah has ever seen.

"How are our supplies? Will they last us to where we are going?" Jeremiah asks Bingley who has lit tobacco into a long wooden pipe and taken a seat next to him.

"Fresh water'll last us three sunsets. I never did travel east of the big island, me boy. Waters are said to be dangerous in these parts, so you best keep yer young eyes peeled for anythin' suspicious like. Me acquaintances back on the Fringey tells me it's not longer than a two-day journey to a little oasis wheres we can fill up our supplieses. I spose if theys were wrong, there's no way of knowing or squaking bout it." Bingley squints his eyes while looking into the distance.

Jeremiah realizes it's not just Quinn who lost everything in the Varthian Fringe. Bingley also had people there. He remembers the giant hugging other people his size at the Jubilee.

"Where is our heading, anyway, Bingley?" Jeremiah asks hoping to avoid the subject. Loss is nothing new to this world and you don't go talking about it unless you are ready for the lineup of devastation in people's past.

"We be going to me home country, Scorton. Said to be isolated past these waters, it'll be our haven. I can't hardly wait to see me fam again. Me mom, she had me in Vathia, ya see, and left me with the Fringeys people before sailing this way... she was a great warrior." Bingley's eyes twinkle with excitement as he explains his life growing up in the Fringe. His big hands help him animate the story of his childhood. Bingley and other orphan giants finding their place with the misfits in the Fringe.

Jeremiah gets taken by his own thoughts. He imagines what Bingley's home island must be like — what creatures live there, what kind of traditions they have, what types of food they eat. His stomach begins to gurgle with hunger and Bingley tosses him some stale bread without missing a word from his story. Quinn begins stirring behind them.

"Good morning, sleepy head." Jeremiah opens his arms to accept a hug from her. She smiles at Bingley from Jeremiah's comfort before vanishing down the stairs, below deck. Jeremiah's fishing rod starts shaking — he's caught something. He battles with the rod, pulling the creature closer to the boat, but not too much so the line doesn't break.

"Bingley, I think I need your help." Jeremiah is almost pulled into the water by his game.

Bingley grabs the rod. "By God! Have a gander at what ya caught."

Jeremiah investigates the water, but only sees darkness. Suddenly, there is a loud sound from under them making the water ripple and separate with bubbles and quakes.

"What's going on?" Jeremiah falls back into the boat.

"Get Quinn up 'ere!" Bingley shouts at Jeremiah, but she has already come up and is screaming at a shadow penetrating the surface. A ship emerges from the water and a wave floods their small boat, sending all of them into the water. Jeremiah's body gets thrown between waves. He doesn't know which way is up. He opens his eyes and sees light shining from above him and a figure swimming to the top. The body of the ship that sank them blocks out the sun, leaving the boy in dark ocean waters.

Jeremiah swims to the back side of the ship. He surfaces with just his head, hoping to remain unnoticed. His eyes burn from the salt water, but he pushes aside the pain. The black ship is dripping wet from being underwater. It has holes in the hull like cannon ball wounds from battle. The sails are ripped almost to shreds and there are mussels and seaweed covering it from top to bottom. It's like a sunken ship just rose up out of the water and is somehow able to sail. A darkness surrounds the ship that makes Jeremiah's chest hurt, but an even more visible darkness surrounds the sky and waters around the ship, like it's in a constant state of storm. Quinn's scream grabs Jeremiah's attention. It's coming from aboard the ship. He grabs onto an overhanging rope to climb the ship, but something grabs onto his foot and drags him back under the water. Jeremiah begins kicking at whatever has a firm hold of his foot in a futile attempt to escape its grasp. It has a long fin for a tail, but a hand that holds onto his foot with great strength, dragging Jeremiah to the hull of the ship where a hole is punctured clean through. How is this boat floating? The creature lets go of Jeremiah and turns to face him. It has two long blue fins and a human head — just like the creature he saw when he first arrived on the Varthian beach. Its upper body is also human, but with dark blue and golden scales. The fingers connect with webbing and it has large gills on its neck. It points to the hole on the hull. Jeremiah doesn't move, he is awestruck by the creature. It creases its golden eyebrows into a frown and changes its eyes from black to red indicating frustration. It pushes Jeremiah towards the ship with its back fins and swims deep into the darkness of the sea. Jeremiah realizes he's been holding his breath for quite some time now and swims to the hull with all his might. As soon as he swims through the hole, he coughs up salty water, lying on dark wooden floorboards in what appears to be a storage room. A crab scurries between gunpowder barrels and through a door that is slightly ajar. The room is dark except for a beam of light coming through the door from the next room. Jeremiah gently lifts his body into the ship, making sure he stays as quiet as possible. He can hear voices in the next room.

"Ye best put 'er in the cell, ya flee-ridden dog, unless ye want our Lord angry wit' ya," a growling voice proclaims.

"Talk ta me like that again and I'll have ya hanging from the mast, ya scoundrel," another voice barks back.

"Unhand me, you, filth." Quinn's voice is shaking through her demanding tone.

Jeremiah crawls to the door to peek out and sees one of the men slap Quinn across the face. There are three men in total. Two of them look identical with long figures and curly black hair. The third can't be taller than five feet with no hair at all. They all have clammy white skin and pitch-black eyes. These are the men of

"...Lord Demetrius," Jeremiah whispers out loud, causing all three men to turn their heads towards him. The smaller man's head turns almost all the way around in an unnatural way. Jeremiah is quick to his feet, looking for some type of weapon to fight the men with. They tie Quinn to a chair and arm themselves with rusty, broken swords. Jeremiah hides behind a crate just as the door opens with a *CREAK*.

"Who be in here? Show yourself at once or face the consequences," one of the taller men threatens with a growl. The smaller man crawls along the ground like a rat with his sword in his mouth. Jeremiah closes his eyes, afraid of being seen. If only he had a weapon to defend himself. Suddenly, a loud whistle sounds and the three men leave the room almost in a trance, closing the door behind them. Jeremiah sighs in relief. He stands up and finds that one of the men left their swords in the room. Quickly arming himself, he opens the door slowly. The men and Quinn are gone. He needs to find her.

Outside the door is a long room filled with hammocks and two tables with chairs. Stairs leading to the deck are located on Jeremiah's left. He hides in the shadows, to get past them undetected. There are at least a dozen hammocks that are empty. The ship smells like mold and stale air. It's almost enough to make Jeremiah sick. There are candles lit throughout the sleeping quarters and the occasional fish flopping along the floor, caught from the ship moving from under the sea to the surface so quickly. He can see steel bars making up two cages at the end of the hammocks. The first cage appears empty except for shackles and a metal bowl with murky water. The second cage contains a large, red-bearded man lying on his side. Jeremiah kneels beside him; afraid he might be dead. He lays his hand on Bingley's shoulder; it feels ice cold. There is a wool blanket in one of the hammocks. Jeremiah feeds it through the cage and lays it gently over his friend.

"I'll get us out of here," Jeremiah whispers to Bingley.

The giant's eyes open wide, but they are not glistening blue. They are pitch black like the depths of the ocean.

"There is no escaping him." Bingley grabs Jeremiah's arm with such force it could have broken in half. Jeremiah reaches for the sword and raises it to chop off his friend's grip.

"If you are in there, Bingley Toppet, come back to me." Jeremiah gives a quick and final warning. Bingley's grip loosens on Jeremiah's arm and his eyes transition back to a faded blue colour. Bingley whimpers and begins shaking. His skin is white and clammy like Lord Demetrius's men.

"Bingley, what's happened to you?" Jeremiah rubs his arm where Bingley's large handprint has left a red mark.

"He's got me soul, ma boy. I'm a goner." Bingley's body jerks and shakes between his whimpering.

"You aren't gone yet, my friend. Don't lose hope." Jeremiah stands up and marches towards the stairs with determination. There is a long, black coat lying on one of the hammocks that he puts on to disguise himself from the crew. He can sense danger above, but that risk is outweighed by his friend's need for him. He is being brave, but more than that; he is fearless.

Chapter 19

The fog that was beginning to set earlier has now
flooded the deck of the ship. Jeremiah can't see two feet
in front of him, but he is determined to find Quinn. He
walks carefully along the uneven floorboards of the
deck, being cautious not to bring unwanted attention to
himself. The deck creaks from his right. He immediately
hides behind an escape boat. A dark figure appears
through the fog, strikes a match and lights up a cigar.
It's a man wearing black boots that are loose on his feet,
making a clunking noise as he paces on the deck. He
wears a dark blue Varthia guard uniform. The pants are
worn out on the knees and the black stripes along the
sides have almost disappeared. A white shirt is
unbuttoned showing dark chest hair and a rusted key.
He is wearing what looks like a Varthian captains'
jacket, but the Crystal Star crest has been torn from
where it normally sits over the heart. Dried blood
splatter covers the uniform. His hair is slicked back into
a tie, but one delinquent piece hangs over his right eye.
The man probably can't see the untamed piece as a
ragged scar runs through the top of his right eye. There
is something about this man that is so familiar yet
frightening to Jeremiah. The man continues pacing back

and forth on the deck, puffing on his cigar. He walks close to Jeremiah's hiding place and leans on the escape boat while looking into the distance. His face looks different from Lord Demetrius's men. It's like he has a soul that is his, not overtaken by the darkness. He tosses half of the cigar into the sea and slicks his hair back with his hand. His face looks anxious and troubled. Jeremiah wonders what he is looking for in the distance. Another man walks through the fog and into view. He is an ugly looking man with missing teeth and white hair that has a tinge of green like seaweed. His eyes are black, surrounded by wrinkly grey skin and he walks with a slouch making him much shorter than the other man. He coughs into his hand and a red liquid stains his pale skin. Blood.

"Pardon my intrusion," the older man says in a frail voice while removing his bandana, showing respect to the other man.

"Speak, Crippen. What word from the men?" The first man crouches to be at eye level with the hunched, older man.

"We've lost him, I'm afraid. Gone back to the sea, we reckon." The man's voice cracks and causes him to cough. The cough of a man with years of tobacco and sea water in his lungs.

"No. He hasn't left. I can feel him." The man closes his eyes and breathes in the air. He turns and looks straight at the boat Jeremiah is hiding behind. Jeremiah is sure he can't see him from where he is hiding, but it still makes his stomach drop. "When the men return, search the boat. He wouldn't leave without her."

"Yes, Lord Demetrius, right away." Crippen turns away and leaves back through the fog. Jeremiah's heart beats faster and faster. The legend that he's heard in stories, myths and warnings. The name that is whispered in the darkest of nights across the seas and the haunter of in-betweens. Jeremiah tightens his grip on his sword and clenches his teeth. Lord Demetrius has turned his back to Jeremiah and lights another cigar while closing his good eye. It would take five seconds for Jeremiah to catch him off-guard and slice him open. He envisions himself as the hero, killing the evil of the seas, avenging so many that have been slaughtered at this man's command. There is something about the way Lord Demetrius is rubbing his brow and looking into the distance that stops Jeremiah. His human tendencies and Jeremiah's curiosity is the only thing stopping the act. There are so many unanswered questions. What would the Lord of the ocean want with Jeremiah? Suddenly, a voice enters his head.

'I know you are here. You are not in danger. When the moon reaches its fullest tonight, meet me at the helm.' Lord Demetrius's eye opens, and he walks away into the fog, out of sight.

Jeremiah holds his hand to his chest and closes his eyes, trying to calm his heart. He feels more weight heavying his body and can't help thinking the darkness on the boat is causing it. He wonders if Lord Demetrius can feel the pain too or if he's numb to the chronic heaviness. The fog begins to lift from the ship, showing that he is the only soul on deck. He needs to decide his next move, but he's stuck between looking for Quinn and waiting to meet Lord Demetrius. Does he risk being caught by the men or does he play into Lord Demetrius's game? The Lord has gone through a lot of trouble to catch Jeremiah and he doesn't think they will hurt Quinn as long as he is still missing. He thinks back to Lord Demetrius looking directly where he was hiding. Did he know he was behind the escape boat all along? Did he want Jeremiah to hear the conversation he was having with Crippen? He needs to see Lord Demetrius. He needs to know why he is looking for Jeremiah. Why it is so important for the conqueror of the sea to hunt down a slave, an outsider, a nobody. He decides to first check on Bingley, hoping that Quinn will be in the empty cage beside him.

Jeremiah creeps across the deck towards the stairs leading down to where his friend is caged. He lays flat on his stomach, using his arms to crawl so that he will remain unseen while peeking down the steps. There is a faint light coming from the hammock room that seems to be flickering. It must be a candle. He crawls down the steps and looks around the corner to the see what is causing the light. A table has been moved into the middle of the hammocks and Crippen is sitting across from a raven. There are small rectangular blocks in front of the bird and the man.

"All righty, you flea-ridden winged demon. I gots a red feather and two blue keys. Only two other tricks can beat THAT." The man shakes in the seat like a nervous dog.

"SQUAWK." The raven almost converses with Crippen, pushing his blocks towards the elder man with his talons. Crippen flips the tiles over to see what the raven has.

"By the full moon's devils! You've been sitting on three bells this entire time? Made a fool by a bird! If it's not my soul lost at sea, it's my mind!" Crippen throws his wrinkled hands in the air and slouches back into his chair. The raven squawks again, takes a small gold chain from the table and flies over Jeremiah's head into the crisp air outside.

Crippen grumbles to himself before walking over to a hammock to lie down. He pulls the bandana from his neck and moves it to cover his eyes. Jeremiah crawls towards the table and waits, hidden from Crippen's sight. He rests his head on the ship's wall, exhaustion begins to set in as the adrenaline fades. He watches the candle's wax drip onto the table, getting smaller and smaller with every passing moment. Jeremiah needs to make sure Crippen is asleep before he can go past him to the cages. He closes his eyes and pictures Crippen's heart beating fast. He can hear Crippen grumbling about losing to a raven, then Jeremiah can hear Crippen thinking about logistics of the block game. Jeremiah has never seen or heard of the block game before, but he somehow understands it from Crippen's thoughts. Suddenly, Crippen's mind turns to blackness. There is only hatred, and evil thoughts of torture and pillaging. A small girl nailed naked to a tree with her bloodied toy doll at her feet. A homeless man beheaded yet still clutching a metal tin he used moments before to peddle. Could these be memories or is it Lord Demetrius's effect on the men? Another image of a woman running out of a burning building with fire climbing her back. She collapses in a scream as it scorches her hair. Jeremiah wishes that Crippen would think of other things. Images of studying in the Librae under a pile of books. Memories in the willows, laughing with Quinn until their stomachs hurt. The woman from the in-between, smiling at Jeremiah and caressing his cheek. He opens his eyes and Crippen is sound asleep, snoring loudly. Jeremiah stands up and sees Crippen is smiling, warmly. If Jeremiah saw what Crippen was thinking, did Crippen see Jeremiah's memories? Did he feel what Jeremiah was feeling? Were the thoughts and feelings translated and did he put the old man fast asleep? Beyond the hammocks, he can see the cages, but they look empty.

"No, no, no!" Jeremiah grabs onto the cold metal bars of the cage that once held his friend captive. The blanket Jeremiah left for the giant lies on the ground near what looks to be a pool of blood. Considering the size of the giant, it's not a deathly amount of blood, but it doesn't instill hope. Jeremiah collapses beside the cage and hangs his head between his knees. Exhaustion and frustration burden his mind and start to break him.

"Get it together, Jer," he whispers to himself while wiping a tear from his cheek. Selfish, annoying and unnecessary emotions when he doesn't know what's truly happened to either of his friends. Bingley has to be alive. Quinn must still be alive, but where on the ship could they possibly be holding them? He stands up and walks back to where Crippen is sleeping. Jeremiah holds his sword to the old man's throat, weighing his options on killing this man. It would be easy. He imagines himself slitting his throat open, spilling enough black blood to cover the floors. He grabs Crippen's sword from his secure holster and places it onto the ground to avoid making noise. Jeremiah closes his eyes and thinks about what Crippen is thinking, again. Instead of rape and torture, he is in the willows. He is inside Jeremiah's memories with a girl who looks like Quinn only much younger. He is laughing and playing hide and seek with the little girl. Jeremiah imagines himself in the dream this time, but out of sight from the two. Crippen's face is fuller with weight, with happiness and with life. He is covering his eyes and counting aloud while the little girl giggles and runs behind a tree. Jeremiah stands out of sight of the other two in the shadows. He watches the girl dodge from tree to tree, playing a game with Crippen only they know. A playful, happy sight. Jeremiah wonders if he can add more to the dream. He imagines a black wolf with piercing yellow eyes. He reaches out and feels its coarse hair, thick and untamed. The wolf growls under its breath, watching the girl and man playing around and waiting for its opportunity. The girl races behind a large willow while Crippen counts again. The growling wolf looks to Jeremiah who nods, sending the wolf to the willow tree. With Crippen's eyes closed, counting, the wolf does its job. Crippen doesn't get to ten before he sees the monster walk away from behind the willow tree where the little girl was hiding, licking its chops. Blood drains thick into the pond, turning it from a crisp blue to crimson. Crippen's face distorts as he realizes what has happened

"Charlie? Charlie, No!" Jeremiah sees Crippen fall onto his knees and scream at the sky. In a mere second, Jeremiah gets a twinge in his chest followed by sharp pain and tears race down his cheeks. What Jeremiah didn't count on, was feeling the pain Crippen is feeling. His chest gets heavy, worse than he's ever felt before. His heart, a black hole sucking his stomach into his throat. Crippen's scream makes Jeremiah's ears ring in a painful way. His knees buckle, and he begins breathing heavier and faster than he's ever done before. The pain is unbearable, he needs the dream to stop. He closes his eyes and imagines the ship again to bring them back out of the in-between. Crippen wakes up screaming while Jeremiah spews stomach bile across the floor. Crippen has tears falling from his blue eyes that fade back to black when he sees Jeremiah. Aware of reality, a most sinister grin creases across Crippen's wrinkly face.

"There y'ar. We been looking all over fer ya, precious," Crippen says in a sinister way that sends chills through Jeremiah's back.

"Wrong. It is I who've found you, Crippen," Jeremiah challenges while drawing his sword. Crippen reaches to where his weapon should be and realizes he has been disarmed. He looks back up at Jeremiah, grinning.

"Clever boy, just like yer father," Crippen says while slowly getting out of the hammock, raising his hands in surrender.

"My father is dead," Jeremiah responds almost with a question. Like most children in this world, Jeremiah was orphaned and has no idea who his parents are.

"Sure, he's dead. Whatever ye say, precious," Crippen responds, grinning at the boy through his few decaying teeth.

"That's enough out of you, move to the deck." Jeremiah shoves Crippen forward, following him up the stairs and to the helm. The moon is shining bright and full for the third night in a row. An anomaly that Jeremiah doesn't have time to theorize.

He shoves Crippen forward again.

"Are you sure yer prepared to meet me Lord?" Crippen asks. Jeremiah doesn't respond. He doesn't have an answer.

How could anyone be prepared to meet Lord Demetrius? The ocean breeze fills his lungs with cold air. He walks up more stairs to the helm where Lord Demetrius is standing with his back to them, puffing on another sweet-smelling cigar. Jeremiah clears his throat to get his attention.

"Hello, my son. Welcome home."

Lord Demetrius turns around slowly and grins at Jeremiah as Crippen scurries back down the steps to the deck.

Chapter 20

Captain Demetrius's black scar almost glistens in the light of the full moon, but not nearly as much as his bright blue eye. You can tell a lot about a person from their gaze. For instance, the captain is facing Jeremiah, but his gaze looks past the boy.

He looks at the horizon instead of into Jeremiah's eyes, like it's a challenge to make eye contact. He is smirking at the boy, but his face is filled with anger and tension. There is something about the way he is looking at Jeremiah that makes him seem trusting, but all Jeremiah knows is the hatred and evil in his soul. The conflict numbs Jeremiah and makes him feel nauseous.

"Did you hear me, Jeremiah?" Demetrius asks with a concerned tone. His voice sounds like it's underwater to Jeremiah as his world becomes dark and he falls to the deck with a thud.

*****

"Jeremiah, wake up, my boy," Anuva whispers into the young boy's ear. The sun trickles through cracks between the barn's wooden walls in Knoen. Jeremiah often fell asleep with the young calves to escape the cold winter chill that his own bed troubles to withstand. The calves are always welcoming of the nine-year-old boy since he brings sugar cubes as an offering for their warmth. Jeremiah opens his eyes and reaches to touch Anuva's cheek with his soft young hand. Anuva brushes Jeremiah's long hair away from his face while admiring how one of the newborn calves is resting on the boy's small stomach.

"What shall we do on your special day, Jeremiah?" Anuva asks. The question brings light into the groggy boy's glistening eyes.

"I thought we weren't allowed to celebrate our birthday?!" the boy asks while wiping his eyes and stretching his small arms out. If it hadn't been for the books in Knoen's Librae, he might not even know what a birthday celebration was.

"And you never bend the rules?" Anuva teases the boy. "If you don't tell anyone and it doesn't take away from your other chores, we could do one special activity. Does that sound like a fair accord to you?"

"Yes, I'll start right away!" Jeremiah gently lifts the calf's head off his stomach and rests it onto a straw pillow before jumping into Anuva's arms. "Thank you, thank you, thank you!" he yells in excitement while running through the barn and out the door. Anuva rubs his face where the boy had touched him. Ascetics don't display affection; it's not appropriate.

Affection leads to feelings and irrational thinking which takes away from their studies. Being aware that your own emotions lead to a self-destructive nature can feel like a betrayal to your own character. It is discipline, and generations of Ascetics secluded on the island practicing phasing out emotions that makes it easier. His family had grown up in Knoen, but he certainly didn't feel the need to touch his father. His mother was not known to him. The women all live in the centre of the island where their duties include gardening, fabric making, reproduction and medical training. They are almost less affectionate than the men and would certainly frown upon Anuva's behavior this winter morning. He is finding it more and more difficult to have Jeremiah as a student and easier to let the boy have control of his feelings, reverting to his human nature. The conflict sits heavy on Anuva's shoulders, but he can't stop himself.

"What are you doing in here?" Isaar interrupts Anuva's thoughts.

"My apologies, Isaar, I didn't hear you enter. I thought I heard noise coming from inside, but there is nothing here." Anuva stands up and bows to the Ascetics' leader.

"I accept your apology, Anuva, but I do not accept lying. I saw the boy run out of here just moments earlier. Now, tell the truth." Isaar's tone doesn't change as the Ascetics practice monotone and rational speaking, but Anuva knows he is unhappy.

Anuva looks down at his feet in silence. He is a terrible liar. Out of practice, mostly.

"I'll take your silence as uncertainty for his whereabouts last night. This isn't his first sleepover with the cattle. I am weary on your task. You were the brightest student, Anuva. I need to be certain you aren't wavering." Isaar's tone still doesn't change when questioning Anuva.

Anuva looks up at Isaar and straightens his back. He read in a book that a straight posture assures confidence. "The boy is doing well. Although he did not sleep in his assigned quarters, I was aware he was here. He finds comfort in the animals. I am confident in my abilities and am training him as you did me."

Isaar looks Anuva in the eyes for an uncomfortable amount of time before responding. "You need to do better than me. The task at hand was too great for any of us to bear. You were chosen because of your intelligence and drive. Disappointment will lead to grave consequences. Failure is not an ending in this book."

"Yes, Isaar, I'm doing my best." Anuva shifts his weight and begins to walk past Isaar.

"You know who you will answer to if you don't complete his task. You know the direct consequences." This sentence has a threatening tone to it. It stops Anuva in his tracks, though he doesn't respond. Isaar clears his throat. "That will be all." Isaar walks past Anuva and disappears into the bright morning sun.

Anuva takes a minute before exiting the barn. He breathes in the crisp air outside. Their winter season doesn't bring snow or extreme cold; only a crispness in the evenings that's enough to harden the grass overnight and cause it to melt in the morning. This amount of wetness in the air makes the honeysuckle intoxicating throughout the island. At this time, nine years ago when they first received Jeremiah, the honeysuckle didn't bloom. Not a single crop grew that winter season. As Anuva walks through the tall apple orchard, he reflects on that day.

A dark ship arrived at their shores, with the tides helping it across the Black Reef as if the waters were being commanded. Isaar was new to leadership and instructed the Ascetics to refrain from confrontation and to gather in the conference hall of the Librae. The skies had been black for almost a week and the grass turned an awful burgundy color from whatever evil was inside the rain. The ship's captain forced his way to the top of the island which wasn't difficult as the Ascetics are a peaceful people. It was the only time they've ever had this type of encounter as intruders are either gobbled by the sea or the Black Reef. Anuva remembers seeing the captain for the first time. He was a handsome man with short black hair and a Varthian uniform that looked brand new. He wasn't accompanied by companions or guards. He carried a basket close to his body. He walked with determination through the crowd of Ascetics without making eye contact with any of them. Anuva felt a heaviness on his chest as the man came closer to him. There was a distinct smell about him that was inviting, yet dangerous. The captain's eyes were bright blue and fixed on the Librae where Isaar was standing. He grinned at the new leader like a lion would at a mouse. An alpha amongst submissive prey, he was devious, and more than that, the Ascetics knew he was pure evil. Isaar opened the door to the Librae and guided the captain in with a bow and a wave of his hand. The Ascetics silently followed them into the building.

"Welcome to the Librae." Isaar greeted the intruder like a guest and escorted him into his study in the back room, shutting the door behind him. Most communities might have started into chaotic panic, but the Ascetics have a procedure for everything. They each take a sitting mat and meditate in the conference hall, waiting for their leader to finish the meeting with the invader.

Moments pass in the silent hall with a quiet dripping from a leak hitting a wooden bucket in an off-beat rhythm. The concrete room has a meter long glass window that lines the back and right-hand side of the walls to display the gloomy looking weather. Anuva found it hard to shut his eyes and meditate. He always struggled to keep his mind blank and consistently found himself distracted by his own worries. What if the captain isn't looking for peace with Isaar? What if he kills him behind that closed door? The Command doesn't have protocol for intruders as it hasn't ever happened, and they aren't due back for at least another month when high tide returns. He imagines his thoughts drifting into the rain outside and washing down the cliffs into the waters, sinking into the depths of the ocean. He wishes he could be simple and ignorant to the side of his brain that questions their existence, questions their purpose.

The door to the study opens and Isaar steps out.

"Anuva, can you come in here, please?" Isaar calls him into the back room where the dark man will be waiting.

Anuva walks past the silent Ascetics and into the room. It's dark inside with the only window covered by a sheet of red fabric and a candle slowly burning to its death. The captain puffs on a cigar and has sat the basket on Isaar's study desk. Anuva takes a seat and nervously fidgets with his shirt collar.

"Anuva, this is Demetrius," Isaar introduces the stranger.

"Lord," the man says, not looking up from the wicker basket.

"My apologies, Lord Demetrius." Isaar's voice wavers. This Lord Demetrius intimidates their leader making Anuva even more uncomfortable with the intruder.

"I hear you are different than the others." Demetrius addresses Anuva with almost a question in his voice.

"Different, how?" Anuva asks.

"Anuva, you don't think like the others. Your sense of rationale isn't solely dependent on intelligence. You rationalize based on the person you are speaking to, based on your environment and on some occasions, based on feelings," Isaar answers.

Anuva feels suddenly hot in the cold room. A secret struggle and a part of his soul has just been revealed to his leader and the intruder. His biggest secret and largest flaw put on display for what? For judgement? He opens his mouth to defend the offensive accusation but is interrupted by Lord Demetrius.

"He will do." The intruder speaks, stands up and begins to open a back door that leads outdoors.

"Sir, when will we see you again?" Isaar calls after him. The Lord stops in his tracks and throws his cigar to the ground outside without turning to face them.

"You won't." The Lord pulls his collar up to cover his neck and disappears into the thick storm.

Thunder rolls outside and Isaar lets out a deep breath before pulling out a container of brown liquid and two glasses from inside his drawer. He pours a little of the liquid into each glass and gives one to Anuva.

"It will help the nerves," Isaar says almost excusing the forbidden liquid while tilting the glass to his mouth.

"Isaar, what am I doing here?" Anuva asks.

"You are an Ascetic and you are here to learn." Isaar pours more liquid into his glass.

"That's not what I meant." Anuva brings the glass to his nose, smelling the liquid. "Is this poison?" He sets the glass back on his table.

"I know what you meant. Drink the liquid first." Isaar swigs his second glass.

Anuva drinks the liquid and coughs half of it back onto his chin. He uses his sleeve to wipe away the drips. Isaar refills Anuva's glass and sits back in his chair.

"Lord Demetrius needs something from us. He needs something from you." Isaar turns the basket towards Anuva. A baby lies in the basket, quietly sleeping. As their world begins to turn upside-down, this infant has found peace.

Anuva drinks the liquid again with less coughing. "Isaar, why did Lord Demetrius give us a baby?" He begins to feel his head getting cloudy and has unclenched his jaw from grinding his teeth.

"Anuva, I need you to not ask questions. I need you to raise this child as I raised you. You need to raise him with intelligence and full knowledge of our world." Isaar pushes the basket towards Anuva.

"I don't know, Isaar. Don't you think…" he pauses, coming up with his thoughts "…wouldn't you be better suited to raise him?"

"This is not open for discussion. He chose you to raise him, not me. If we deviate, he will know, and he will be back." Isaar's voice changes from demanding to uncertainty. There is panic in his voice, but more alarming is the fear in his eyes. "You must raise him, Anuva. You must train him for he will follow in his father's footsteps," Isaar says while pouring them another glass.

"But, Isaar, it's not my time to raise a child, yet. I don't even know how," Anuva protests the decision again.

"No more debate! Take the child, Anuva, and get out of my sight." Isaar slams his glass onto the desk causing it to shatter. Red trickles from Isaar's shaking fist onto the wooden desk.

Anuva takes the child and turns to go out the back door.

"One more thing, Anuva. He must never know how he got here or where he came from. This is important." Isaar begins to cover his cut with some torn fabric from his drawer.

"What do I even call him?" Anuva asks feeling muscled into a decision. It's not in his nature to challenge the Ascetic's leader, but fear will make you question a lot of things.

"His name will be Jeremiah," Isaar responds.

"Meaning *Exaltation of the Lord.*" Anuva strokes the baby's soft arm before opening the door to leave. The skies have cleared, and the heaviness Lord Demetrius brought with him lifts from the island.

Chapter 21

Most ships creak while they sail through the sea. It's an aching sound, a struggling moan as it cuts through the current. *Hades Pride* sails without noise. She carves through the sea like a knife through soft butter. Her torn sails and broken hull offend reason. It should be at the bottom of the ocean, but something else is keeping it afloat. Something that can't be seen or heard but can be felt heavy on your chest. The raven who outwitted Crippen sits in a room below deck. His right eye is closed and scarred, causing it to be blind. He sits watch over a sleeping Jeremiah. A soft yellow light begins to pierce the darkness of night. It catches the raven's good eye. He caws loudly until the boy begins stirring and then flies through the broken window into the dawn.

Jeremiah opens his eyes to take in his surroundings. The deepness of his in-between makes his head foggy. He is in a finely decorated room with paintings, red drapes over the broken window and a matching red bedspread with gold trimmings. He rubs his eyes and tries to remember where he is. His right hand reaches to his heart as the heaviness reminds him. Somehow, he's been changed into a white nightgown that smells like it's been in a musty closet for years. How long has he been asleep? He shoves the blankets off his legs and stands to have a better look around. A painting grabs his attention. A woman stands near a tree with a baby in her hands. Her chocolate eyes match her skin, dark like the tree she stands under. She is dressed in attire much like Quinn's people. The child is covered by linens except his hand which is holding onto her hair. Jeremiah feels a strange attachment to them. There is something desperately beautiful about the way she is looking at the infant, a rare jewel to the woman. He knows that mothers have loving tendencies, from seeing them outside of Knoen, but the concept is still foreign to Jeremiah. The obvious bond in the mother's eyes brings a peacefulness to Jeremiah that he'd only felt with Quinn. It would be too easy to describe it as love, because it wasn't just a likeness or infatuation. There was a soul connection; a bond to the heart and an understanding that can only be felt.

He shakes his head to release his thoughts from the painting. He needs to focus on finding a weapon before someone comes to check on him. He opens drawers on a dresser and finds they are empty. There are two tables on either side of the bed, but they are both empty as well. A table sits at the end of the bed covered with a red cloth and roses inside a gold vase. There is also a small silver hand mirror that looks to be intact. Jeremiah lifts the tablecloth, but there is nothing under the table. They must have cleared the room already. His clothes are folded on the opposite side of the bed from where he was sleeping. He quickly puts them on and grabs the mirror to have a look at himself. He tries to remember the last time he saw his reflection before lifting the mirror to his face. The man looking back is barely recognizable. His facial hair has grown out more and his hair is getting longer than he likes to keep it. The biggest change is in his eyes that have developed dark circles underneath them and the irises themselves have changed from blue to a smoky grey.

The bedroom door swings open with such force that it causes Jeremiah to drop the mirror. It shatters into pieces as soon as it hits the ground. A strong wind howls into the room, sending thousands of little chills down his back. Jeremiah walks to the door and peeks outside. He quickly realizes he is in the captain's quarters. Outside of the room is a very busy deck.

Captain Demetrius's men have returned. He recognizes the three men he encountered when he first arrived on the ship. They are arranging other giant men into a line. They must have captured them on a pillage. The short one with the bald head turns to Jeremiah's direction, smiles, and gives a two-finger wave before turning back and hitting one of the captured men in the stomach with the butt end of a sword. Jeremiah walks out into the light of the morning and takes in the workings of the ship. He starts counting Demetrius's men, but loses track after fifteen. Two men are securing the transport ships back onto the deck. Another three are climbing ropes on the mast almost in competition to get

163

to the crow's nest. There is one man singing while swabbing the deck, hips swaying from side to side as he sings into the mop handle. Jeremiah can't hear what he is singing over the other men speaking, shouting and working. He spots Crippen in the middle of the deck. He is speaking to a man that stands quite tall but has his back to Jeremiah. It's hard for Jeremiah to see in between men moving their stolen spoils to different places on the ship. Crippen points to Jeremiah and the man turns around to look at him. He is an older man with strong features and grey streaks in his hair. The man does the same two-finger wave with his left hand, revealing a Tradey mark on his wrist. Jeremiah has a flashback to the man who was speaking to Charlotte at the Jubilee Celebration. With his large hooded coat and treasonous marking; it must be the same man.

"It's a fascinating sight, isn't it?" Jeremiah is startled by Lord Demetrius who has appeared beside him. He marvels at his men working, a God watching over his people.

"Our definitions of fascinating are slightly different." Jeremiah looks up at Demetrius, waiting for him to bite back. The Lord grins slightly. Amused by Jeremiah's retaliation.

"We aren't that different, you and I," he says while nodding to Crippen and the man from the Fringe. They sneer at Jeremiah, but he pays no attention to them.

"You and I are nothing alike," Jeremiah corrects Demetrius.

"Don't assume to know so much about me. After all, my blood runs thick through your veins." He reaches out to grab the hand of the man from the Fringe. "Victor, do you have the account of our spoils? It appears to have been a successful enough pillage." The man carries a notebook and pencil with him. He has a way of carrying himself that is unlike the rest of the crew. His eyes are still jet black with Lord Demetrius's curse, but he is more than just a black-hearted Tradey. He is distinguished in the way that wealth and education can make you. He opens his book to a place that's been saved with a red ribbon.

"1,000 in coin, 50 pieces of jewels and fifteen men. We lost only one creature and three men, Lord Demetrius, sir." He closes the book, slips his pen behind his ear and slides his hand through his wavy hair.

"Well done, Victor. That's a nice amount of men collected considering the brute of Scorton." Lord Demetrius rests his hand on Victor's arm.

"Scorton? That's where Bingley is from," Jeremiah says, but neither of the men acknowledges that he's spoken. Flashes of Bingley's people being beaten and killed enter Jeremiah's head.

"Where is Bingley?" Jeremiah asks, but is blatantly ignored again. "Lord Demetrius, I demand to know where my friends are this instant," Jeremiah yells.

The ship falls silent. Lord Demetrius's men stop dead in their tracks and stare at Jeremiah with hateful eyes. Some of them slide their weapons out of holsters and others arm themselves with whatever wood or iron is around.

"Jeremiah, I would like to show you something." Lord Demetrius doesn't look at Jeremiah but rests his hand on the boy's back as if escorting him forward. Jeremiah is still being glared at. He looks at his feet like an ashamed boy being scolded by his parent.

"Back to work," Lord Demetrius commands his men with a backward wave of assurance to them. They put their weapons away, obeying the Lord's orders. Jeremiah lied earlier. The amount of control and authority the Lord has over the men is beyond fascinating. Lord Demetrius leads Jeremiah to the lineup of Scorton captives. They are very large men just like Bingley, but certainly he must be an anomaly as Jeremiah distinctly remembers him standing much taller than Lord Demetrius's captured men. They stand silently, looking at their feet. All that is, except one. This man stands taller and stronger than the rest. He stares straight ahead, not at his feet and not at Lord Demetrius, but off into the distance. Lord Demetrius walks past them like a Varthian Master surveying his slaves. He stops at the strong man, eyeing him up and down.

"What would your name be?" Lord Demetrius asks.

"Taverence Garvia, ambassador of the free world and leader of the Scorton army," the man says without blinking or changing his gaze. Lord Demetrius grins his most cunning of grins.

"Impressive," he admits, which draws sneers from his men. "And who do you believe I am, Taverence of Scorton?" Lord Demetrius asks the man, clearly toying with him.

"You'd be Lord Demetrius, the enemy of the free world." Taverence falls into Lord Demetrius's game.

The Lord makes a disapproving sound with his tongue and shakes his head. He continues walking the line, touching the men as he walks. He grabs one man's face to get a better look at him, another man he pushes on his shoulders to make him stand straight. "I am who you say, however, I am not your enemy, Taverence of Scorton. The Command is your enemy and Varthia is her home. I am here to offer you freedom, to break the chains and to liberate you."

"Lord Demetrius, the Liberator." Lord Demetrius moves his hands like a conductor as his men repeat the phrase three times over. Jeremiah is awestruck. None of the men move or even look up from their duties while chanting the phrase.

"You are a destroyer. You bring destruction and chaos, not freedom." Taverence speaks up again. Jeremiah nods his head, agreeing with the man.

"You aren't getting it, Taverence of Scorton," Lord Demetrius says while resting his arm on the man's shoulder. "I am the means to an end. For too long the Command has poisoned these waters with its rules, with its reform. For too long it's separated families, enslaved thousands and controlled innocent people. What is the free world doing for that?"

"Well, we… we are…" Taverence struggles to answer.

"Scorton does nothing but sit in its blissful island, hundreds of kilometers away from any other and out of the clutches of the Command," Lord Demetrius answers for him. He begins addressing the rest of the men, "You sit here on your island, isolated in my waters from Varthia. Well, this land of milk and honey belongs to everyone under the Command's thumb and not just to your people. It's our duty to free the rest of the world from Varthia's Command, will you help me?" Lord Demetrius directs the question to Taverence.

The rest of the captured look at Taverence, looking for him to respond, but he simply hangs his head down in defeat.

"I offer you a place, nay, a home and a purpose. You will join my fight; you will help with the destruction and chaos and you will be liberated." Lord Demetrius looks to Jeremiah with a dark, amused smile.

His men begin chanting the phrase again, "Lord Demetrius the Liberator." The skies have turned dark and rain begins to drop onto the deck.

Now, I promise this will hurt, but I also promise that it will only last a moment." Lord Demetrius walks over to Taverence and holds his hand to his heart.

"What will hurt?" Taverence asks, but too late. Jeremiah can see the Lord's eye change from ocean blue to jet black, completely consuming both iris and white sclera. Taverence's body lifts off the ground and the large man moans in pain. His shirt rips open from the wind that's picked up and the rest of the men can see his chest turning black from where Demetrius's hand is resting on his heart. The black spreads throughout his body, traveling through his veins. Taverence's moans turn into screams as the black has made its way through his neck and into his face. Lord Demetrius has tilted his head to the side as if to amplify the transformation. A boom of thunder sends Jeremiah's stomach into his heart.

"Enough!" Jeremiah finds himself shouting instinctually at the painful and torturous screams coming from Taverence. Suddenly, the man begins to lower back to the ground and his screams have changed back into slight moans, like a whimpering dog. Lord Demetrius's eye turns blue again and he rubs his hand from where it was placed on Taverence's chest. The rest of the men in the line look at Taverence as if expecting something about him to change.

"Taverence, say something," one of the men in the line asks. Jeremiah doesn't turn to see who. He wants to see what has happened to the giant of a man.

"What is your name?" Lord Demetrius asks Taverence.

"Taverence of Scorton," he responds to the Lord.

"And do you know who I am?" Lord Demetrius asks while pacing through the lineup of Scorton men.

"Lord Demetrius, leader of the free world. The Liberator," Taverence yells above the storm, pushing his fist into the air. The rest of Lord Demetrius's men yell in approval of their new comrade.

Lord Demetrius begins touching the rest of the men, initiating their transformation. Jeremiah is speechless watching them change from normal men into dark thugs, men of Lord Demetrius. As the final transformation happens, Lord Demetrius walks to Jeremiah.

"Impressed, yet?" he asks him. Jeremiah simply shakes his head, but not as a no. He shakes his head in a speechless, astonished and awed way. Lord Demetrius reaches into his pocket and produces two cigars for him and Jeremiah.

"There is no way this is right," Jeremiah argues almost with himself.

"Ah yes, but who is to say what is right and wrong?" Lord Demetrius responds. But all Jeremiah can do is shake his head. He knows what the Command has done and has experienced their evil first-hand. They must be stopped, but at what cost? The men Lord Demetrius changed have blended in with the other dark workers, transporting bags to the cargo hold and tying down ropes.

"Would you care to join me for dinner later?" Lord Demetrius changes the topic.

"I'll have to check my schedule." Jeremiah's response has Lord Demetrius chuckling. He wraps his arm around Jeremiah's shoulder and places his captain's hat onto Jeremiah's head. They stand in silence as the storm mysteriously fades away.

Chapter 22

The open sea has always been Jeremiah's favourite smell. On the islands, there is a hint of fish on the breeze from decaying ocean life on the shore. Deep in the ocean, you get a true fresh sea smell that makes the heaviness on his chest feel lighter. He closes his eyes and breathes in deeply, filling his lungs with the ocean breeze. He holds his breath for as long as possible, getting his fill of the smells and tastes that come with the air. Victor shows up beside Jeremiah while he is practicing his deep breathing, scaring the sea air out of his lungs in a coughing fit. Lord Demetrius left Jeremiah directly after transforming the Scorton men. Jeremiah hasn't left the ship deck, watching the men work and enjoying the fresh air.

"It takes a lot out of him." Victor talks about Lord Demetrius while walking the deck with Jeremiah. "He makes sure that the task looks easy, but he always sleeps for hours afterwards and a large meal follows. A dinner he usually attends alone, but I hear you be joining him." He almost questions Jeremiah as if getting confirmation of the rumor.

"Yes, he invited me," Jeremiah confirms.

"You must be special, boy. Not many enter this ship without being transformed and no one has ever eaten with the Lord since I've been his first." Victor walks with his chest puffed out as if it's full of air.

"I suppose it's because I'm his son," Jeremiah confesses. Victor smiles and nods his head. He doesn't seem surprised by the fact. "How do you know Charlotte?" Jeremiah asks which does surprise Victor. "I saw you talking with her at the Crystal Jubilee." He studies Victor, determining how the man reacts to being caught off-guard.

"Clever boy." Victor smiles at Jeremiah. "How did you know that was me?"

"I recognized your coat. That and the mark on your wrist." Jeremiah points to Victor's left arm. The man lifts his sleeve to reveal the mark. He strokes it with his hand, almost like he's trying to rub it off and then covers it just as quickly.

"Yes, that was a long time ago. I don't remember my life before…"

"Before Lord Demetrius took you," Jeremiah interjects.

This makes Victor hesitate in his story and look out into the distance. There is only water surrounding the ship as far as the eye can see. Jeremiah struggles with what to say. He wants to know everything but is wary of what is safe to ask.

"Have you learnt nothing from being here? I was taken as threateningly as a child is taken from his

173

mother's womb. I may not remember what my life was before, but Lord Demetrius freed me and gave my life purpose." Victor shakes his head. "You should give your father a chance."

"How can you say that? You may have been a king before for all you know," Jeremiah argues. Victor rolls his sleeve up again and puts his wrist in Jeremiah's face.

"Look at this. You know just as well as I what this means. I may not remember, but I am reminded every day that I was an outcast before."

A vein creeps its way down Victor's forehead showing his annoyance of the interrogation.

"I have just one more question," Jeremiah tells the man. "What were you doing in the Fringe? Why did you send those creatures in?" Victor's eyebrows rise in confusion. Jeremiah realizes he already knows the answer to the question. "You were looking for me."

"Your father has been tracking you for as long as any of us can remember." Victor smiles at Jeremiah. "Charlotte alerted us as soon as you arrived on the Fringe."

Jeremiah retraces his time at the Fringe. How long had Charlotte known he was the son of Lord Demetrius?

"Allow me to show you around the ship." Victor changes the subject and holds his hand out as if asking Jeremiah to walk ahead of him.

"The men in the crow's nest are keeping a keen eye out for other ships to take and, more importantly, they watch for the Command. *Hades Pride* is out of the Command's reach, its speed and ability to change direction is unmatched. We still run into the odd Tradey ship and if we are lucky, a Command ship. There are a handful of men under the deck, organizing the spoils. It may seem ridiculous for cursed men to keep spoils, but Lord Demetrius promised to lift us from our duties as soon as we take the Command and Varthia with it. It's important we have the means to live out the remainder of our lives," Victor explains using his hands to point out the men. "The rest of the men are either sleeping in the bunks or they are playing a game that Crippen made up and Lord Demetrius's raven usually wins." Victor chuckles to himself thinking of Crippen losing to the raven. His laugh is deep, from his stomach.

Jeremiah is stunned. He thought Lord Demetrius's men were all soulless creatures, but that's not the case. They have real thoughts; they need food, water and rest. They are still human.

"Oh, I almost forgot! There is also Cookie who naturally, is the cook." Victor licks his lips. "I could only imagine what kind of meal that man has for you tonight. He also has a Tradey mark. Found him just off Varthia not long before we picked you up."

Jeremiah has glimpses of Cookie in his head. He decides not to tell Victor that he knows the Tradey from the transport that shipwrecked him into the Fringe. It wouldn't do any good and it's not like Cookie would remember him.

"Jeremiah?" Victor waves his hand in front of the boy's eyes, trying to get his attention.

"Sorry, I was just thinking." Jeremiah realizes he'd gotten lost in his own thoughts. Victor smiles at the boy. His short curly hair dances in the ocean breeze and his black eyes almost look dark blue in the sunlight. He has a smile that seems genuine in comparison to other distinguished men that Jeremiah has met. Jeremiah wonders what type of man Victor was before and what he did to earn the Tradey mark.

"Perhaps you should rest before your dinner. It's been a busy day and I'm sure you have much to think about," Victor suggests, and Jeremiah welcomes the idea. Victor guides Jeremiah to the captain's quarters.

"Isn't Lord Demetrius sleeping here?" Jeremiah asks. Victor holds a finger to his lips, motioning for Jeremiah to be quiet. He then points up to the helm where Lord Demetrius sits with his feet up on a stool and his captain's hat over his face. He holds a white cloth in his hand like a handkerchief that is stained red. Jeremiah is reminded of Demetrius coughing red into his hand when he first saw him on the ship's deck. Jeremiah mouths 'thank you' to Victor before disappearing into the room. The mirror that was once shattered has been cleaned and a new one sits on the desk. Jeremiah reaches to pick it up but takes his hand back at the last second. He doesn't want to know what he looks like. He doesn't want to see himself. He strips off his clothes and climbs into the freshly made bed. The events of the morning weigh heavy on his mind, but the struggle to stay awake and toil with his thoughts are overcome by his exhaustion. He quickly falls into a deep sleep where he gets to see her once more.

*****

It always seems to start off as a bright sunny day in Jeremiah's in-between so it is no shock that he feels nearly blinded by the brightness. He sits up and sees a girl beside him. She is fast asleep on a bed of soft grass. She has the same face and features as the woman that usually greets Jeremiah in his in-between, but she looks much younger now. Her skin resembles the bark of a tree and her hair is brown like a chestnut. He reaches out and touches the girl's arm. He expects it to be rough like a tree, but instead it's soft and smooth like skin. She wakes up and smiles at the boy.

"Hello there, what's your name?" the girl asks while sitting up into a yawn and stretch.

Jeremiah is stunned — this is the first time that he's spoken to the woman who is now a girl. Her dress has changed into a half shirt that barely covers her belly button and a skirt. It shows off her muscular figure and small frame.

"I'm Jer… who are you?" Jeremiah asks nervously.

The girl giggles at him. She stands up and quickly ties her hair into a long braid. "My name is Sam," she says while extending her hand out to Jeremiah. The way

177

she does this seems unnatural; like a handshake is more to appease him than it is her first instinct. "I am... pleased to make your acquaintance," she says slowly like she is searching for the exact wording. It's a greeting that isn't natural to her. One she is clearly mimicking from something or someone. Jeremiah stands up and takes her hand. She shakes it with playful exaggeration. He laughs at her and she giggles back, covering her mouth in embarrassment. There is something endearing about her childlike reactions.

"I've never understood the formal greetings, but Dee taught me how your people do it," Sam explains while nervously playing with her hair. Even with a braid, her hair reaches down to her lower back.

"I've never been a fan of formalities," Jeremiah says while smiling at the girl. She giggles again and takes his hand into hers.

"Jer, I'd like to show you something," she says with eyes filled with excitement. He grabs her hand, and she begins running through the meadow. He does his best to keep up with her, but she is quick and graceful. They run past the meadow and through a stream filled with crystal clear spring water. The cool water pricks his feet, but he is only concentrating on keeping up with Sam and not letting her hand slip from his. They approach a forest and don't slow down on their run. She looks back at Jeremiah, smiling at him. Her brown eyes have honey flecks that seem to glisten simply from her happiness. The world slows down for Jeremiah as he is entranced by her innocence and purity. She hasn't been tainted by the world but trusts and loves and laughs without fear. A birch tree appears just in front of them.

"Sam, watch out!" Jeremiah yells, but she runs straight into the tree. He lets go of her hand and stands in bewilderment. The tree swallowed Sam.

"Let go of her!" Jeremiah shouts while hitting the tree with a branch from the ground. "Give her back!" The branch snaps across the tree and a giggling noise catches Jeremiah's ear. Sam appears from behind the tree, amused with herself. "How did you do that?" Jeremiah asks, breathing heavily.

"I am a Spryte. Haven't you seen a Spryte before?" she asks. Jeremiah shakes his head no to her, admiring how her skin changed to match the white tree and is now fading back to its original colour. He had seen a Spryte from afar but hadn't seen this trick. She holds her arm up to the birch tree and runs it through the trunk from back to front, showing the transformation again. Her tanned arm changes to white and grey like the birch and magically switches back when her arm is through the tree.

"How is this possible?" Jeremiah asks, holding Sam's arm.

She simply giggles at his curiosity.

"You haven't seen anything, yet," the girl says to Jeremiah with sparkling eyes. She guides him through the terrain of the forest and eventually to the biggest tree Jeremiah had ever seen. Its trunk width is nearly five times his size and the branches reach high into the sky. If Sam told Jeremiah that they reached the sun, he would believe her. Then again, he would believe anything she told him. At the base of the tree are two blue flowers with petals that reach bigger than Jeremiah's palm. Sam sits on her knees next to the flower and motions for Jeremiah to join her. He sits next to her and waits for her to speak.

"Do you want to see my next trick?" she asks Jeremiah in almost a rhetorical way. She is smiling at him, but in a different way than she had before. There is something sinister in the corner of her mouth. He nods yes anyways. Curiosity has always gotten him in trouble. She closes her eyes for what seems like five minutes, but anticipation has a funny way of affecting your perception of time. When her eyes open, they are pitch-black instead of warm brown. She tilts her head at Jeremiah and smiles her most menacing of smiles before touching one of the flowers. Its royal blue colour fades to black from where Sam touched it. The flower wilts into an ash — like substance in a matter of seconds before Jeremiah's eyes. Sam closes her eyes almost like she's turning off whatever darkness she summoned.

"How can you turn it off and on like that?" Jeremiah asks Sam.

"You've seen it before? I should have known." Sam doesn't seem to know how to stop smiling. Whatever her feelings, she has a smile for it. This time, she wears an inquisitive smile.

"I think I can do it," Jeremiah says to her and closes his eyes to try and mimic her trick.

"You have to clear your mind, Jer. You have to think of what means the absolute most to you; a relative, a friend, a memory... anything!" She coaches him along.

"What if I don't have any of those things? What if what means most to me has already been taken?" Jeremiah asks. He doesn't have his eyes open, but he knows she is smiling at him.

"Then think of what it felt like to lose those things. I want you to think of the people who took those things from you and I want you to take that hatred and dwell in it. Keep it at the front of your mind and don't let anything else disrupt the feeling... the heaviness," she instructs him. Images of Quinn being tortured by Trish and Lord Demetrius's men flash in front of his eyes. Next are images of Bingley being stabbed in the cage by Crippen. Finally, Anuva enters his mind and images of him sending away a young Jeremiah. This time there is no sorrow in Anuva. He wants to send Jeremiah away to be a slave... he may even take some delight in it. Jeremiah opens his eyes and can see the blue flower through black pupils. He touches the tree instead of the flower and it instantly engulfs in the blackness.

"Jer, that's enough!" Sam yells at Jeremiah, but somehow can't get through to him. The darkness has taken over his thoughts. Sam puts her hand over Jeremiah's on the tree and the black becomes white in

181

an explosion of light. It sends Jeremiah onto his back. "Jer, are you okay?" Sam touches his face to wake him.

"My name is Jeremiah." He opens his eyes and tells her. "I never cared for Jer." Sam giggles at his response.

"Well, I never really cared for Sam, either," she says while fixing her hair. "My name is Samara."

*****

Black ooze seeps from Jeremiah's trembling lips and onto the white cotton pillow that has been his only solace since he arrived on *Hades Pride*. He wipes away the blackness as if it was drool. He clasps his hand around the red duvet and pulls it off his muscular body. There is a feeling at the pit of his stomach that sends a cool sensation down to his toes. He's been forgetting something. He grabs for where his drab clothes were while rubbing away the strangeness of his in-between. When he brings the clothes to his view, he can see they are different. In place of old, dingy clothes from the Fringe is a Varthian uniform. It appears to have been freshly washed and smells like the ocean breeze with a hint of vanilla. He smiles big, trying to remember the last time he'd worn anything this nice. In fact, he doesn't remember ever having almost new clothes. The Ascetics didn't wear anything that would display the Varthian Star and Gregor would never have allowed Jeremiah to look better than he. He finishes off the uniform by using a real leather belt to hold the pants in place. He grabs the mirror to look at himself in his new uniform and knocks his carving knife off the small side table. It hits the ground with a bang, demanding his attention. He wraps his hands around the grip, and it causes the aching, forgetting feeling to creep back into his legs. The bed catches him before the floor does and he strokes his beard, trying to remember what he's forgotten.

Jeremiah looks towards the door to see the captain smiling at him.

"How long have you been there?" Jeremiah asks as a smile makes its way into his eyes. Captain Demetrius smiles back at his son in a way that makes Jeremiah forget that he was forgetting something.

"Not very long. The uniform suits you well. I could have guessed we were around the same size. Stand up, let me get the full look at you." His hands beckon for Jeremiah to show off the uniform. Jeremiah abides the man's wish, almost jumping to his feet. The captain raises his forefinger on his knuckle to his chin. "My, does it ever suit you. I wonder if being Captain Demetrius's son would benefit you as a Varthian officer." He laughs, thinking of the mere idea.

Jeremiah laughs too. "I bet they'd lock me in irons and behead me where I stood." They stand smiling at each other for moments before a scowl crosses Jeremiah's face.

"What's wrong, son?" Lord Demetrius asks while resting a hand on Jeremiah's shoulder.

"I know I'm forgetting something, but I can't remember." Jeremiah rubs his head as if he could massage the memory of his lost friends back into his mind, but they are gone. Bingley's happy spirit and Quinn's gentle love are replaced by a father Jeremiah didn't know he needed. His longing for love and family are outweighing the good in his heart. Worse still, Lord Demetrius knows and is pleased beyond measure. Years of cunning plans coming together as the final pieces fall into place.

"Cookie has made quite the feast for us. What say you? Do you have anything else pressing this eve?" Demetrius breaks Jeremiah's thoughts. He looks up at the Lord who stands mere inches taller than he.

"Cookie? What a strange name." Jeremiah scoffs at a man he once knew all too well. They continue out of the captain's chambers and the heaviness Jeremiah once felt is numbed. It won't be long before the darkness consumes him.

Chapter 23

There's something funny your body does when hunger is not a temporary gurgle in your stomach, but instead a chronic and constant absence. One that your body adjusts to; becomes numb to. It's not that the pain subsides, but it becomes a part of you. The pain becomes a state of being.

Jeremiah didn't realize he had become this way until he reached the door to the dining room and caught the aroma of a hot meal inside. He closes his eyes and breathes it all in. Fried seafood, baked cheese and something far different than he'd ever smelt before with a sweetness to it that made saliva drip down the side of his mouth. He uses the back of his right hand to wipe away the drips that laid rest in his untamed beard before squeezing the golden doorknob, letting himself into the dining room.

Not a drop of natural lighting could be seen inside. Oversized, Victorian red drapery mask the small portholes.

Hundreds of candles, small and large, provide an intimate and unexpected ambience that looks out of place considering the state of the ghost ship. A fire is tucked away in the corner, with Lord Demetrius putting another log on the embers while balancing a glass of wine. He smiles at Jeremiah and takes long strides to greet him, snatching a second glass from the table. Handing the glass to Jeremiah, he lifts his own up and holds it out towards the boy. Jeremiah hesitates before tapping his glass onto Lord Demetrius's. He holds the glass to his lips to take a sip but finds himself hesitating again. Lord Demetrius takes a big drink before noticing that his son isn't. He chuckles. "It's not poison. Trust me, if I wanted you dead, I would have done it already."

Jeremiah sets the glass down without sipping it. He knew he'd have a hard time trusting Lord Demetrius, but he never imagined he'd have a hard time not trusting him. The man is a legendary tyrant with a reputation for heinous and evil acts, but his charm masks these facts. An awkward few moments pass as Lord Demetrius takes his place at the head of the six-seated table. Even at the dinner table the man wears the same Varthian uniform, blood stains and all. He studies Jeremiah and Jeremiah studies him right back. A standoff that lasts for an uncomfortable amount of time. Lord Demetrius opens his mouth to say something but is interrupted by Cookie entering the room from a swinging door by the fireplace.

"Foods up, ma Lord," the man says. Jeremiah knows him. He recognizes the man's limp, a twitch just beneath his right eye and the Tradey mark. He can't place him though and as soon as the ex-Tradey drops the fully cooked meal onto the table and limps back into the kitchen, Jeremiah has forgotten again.

The dinner plates on the table are filled with a cooked bird, dinner rolls and all the fixings. Lord Demetrius sips his wine and watches Jeremiah fill his plate and devour the food in front of him like a puppy eating kibble.

"Slow down, son, or you'll be sick," He instructs the boy to little effect.

Jeremiah barely hears Lord Demetrius over his full mouth, chewing food he hasn't tasted since he doesn't even know when. He remembers the Fringe and the Jubilation dinner, but never tried any of the food. He was too busy doing something, but what was it? What was he so busy with that he hadn't had time to eat? He stops and looks at the food, looks at Lord Demetrius and can't remember.

"If you could ask me any one question, what would it be?"

Lord Demetrius lights up a cigar, filling the already smoky room with eucalyptus and tobacco.

Jeremiah swallows down his food and contemplates the question. What one question could cover the multitude of other answers he wants. His cunning mind steps in and speaks the question, hardly missing a beat.

"Why did you leave me on Knoen?" he asks and begins licking the chicken grease off his fingers.

Lord Demetrius looks at Jeremiah disappointedly. This wasn't the question he expected of his son. He takes a long puff from his cigar before answering. "I couldn't very well take a baby with me on my mission."

"My question wasn't about you leaving me. I've been neglected, betrayed, sold, bought, beaten and disowned like every other child of this world. What I'm asking is why Knoen? Why the Ascetics?" Jeremiah relaxes back onto his chair.

This makes Lord Demetrius smile. This is a question worthy of the son of the conqueror of the sea. "I was after the free world, Varthia's world, and what better place to hide my most prized possession than right under my enemies' nose? The Ascetics may live on an island governed by the Command, but they're prisoners of knowledge. Their loyalties lie with their studies and the Librae. A baby isn't out of the ordinary for them nor would they ever hand you over to the Command. A funny thing happens when you become complacent in your tyranny; those you trust the most might just be harboring your biggest weapon. What I didn't count on was them selling you over to the Tradeys. That's when I lost you."

Jeremiah nods silently and takes a cigar from a cherrywood box in the middle of the table. He uses a candle to light it and inhales deeply. He'd snuck some away from Gregor on Jopwen before.

"Am I allowed another question?" Jeremiah asks after silently assessing Lord Demetrius's answer.

A knock at the entry door followed by Victor interrupts their conversation.

"Begging your forgiveness, ma Lord. I've received word from her. Might I speak with you in private?" The distinguished man holds the door for Lord Demetrius to exit without a word.

Jeremiah gets up to stretch. He should have listened to Lord Demetrius. The food he inhaled sits like a rock on his stomach. A painting hanging above the fireplace catches Jeremiah's attention. It's the woman from Jeremiah's in-between, but much younger and she's lying in the wildflower meadow. The likeness is uncanny, making Jeremiah wonder who painted the picture. It's almost like someone grabbed a snapshot of Jeremiah standing over her in his in-between, looking at her from above and transposed it into this frame. He grabs the painting from the wall, turning it around in a fury of curiosity of who painted it. The reverse shows nothing but the back of a canvas. He hangs it back up on the wall only to notice a shadow. The picture is worn, but there is the darkness of a figure moving on her face, getting bigger and bigger.

"Would you like to know about Samara?" Lord Demetrius asks, startling Jeremiah. The boy nods and holds his breath.

Chapter 24

"I want you to close your eyes, Jer. May I call you Jer?" Lord Demetrius instructs. Jeremiah sits on the edge of his seat, nodding at his father.

"I will keep it simple and straight for you," Lord Demetrius begins, and Jeremiah's dark world suddenly illuminates with colour. With his eyes closed, he can see a bright summer day and feel the sun on his face.

Lord Demetrius continues, "I was once in the slave-trade like you a long time ago. I worked for the leader of a fishing tribe off the coast of Varthia. Not on the island itself, but about fifty nautical miles north. Far enough away for the temperatures to reach an uninhabitable cold, where sun was a rare and sought-after commodity." Jeremiah sees the island. Its ice reef sends chills down his spine.

"Between the Tradey beatings and the odd visit from a bloodthirsty Varthia officer, I was never without limp or bruising. I watched too many child slaves suffer from their injuries and a handful even dying from the beatings of Tradey men with no regard for life or innocence. Conditioned from the moment they were plucked off their own home islands as children themselves to be beaters, molesters and adult Tradey slaves of the Command." Jeremiah squirms in his seat as he sees the shadow of a Tradey beating a boy with the business side of a mop, breaking it over the child's body. Memories of his own interactions with a Tradey's temper re-enact in his mind.

"With a sorry excuse for an escape boat and the shirt on my back, I escaped at dawn while the Tradeys were celebrating a big swordfish catch with enough rum to burn down Varthia." Lord Demetrius pauses his story to take a puff of his cigar. Jeremiah considers asking why he didn't take any of the kids with him but isn't sure he would have either. It sounds cutthroat, maybe even cruel but that's the world they live in. Survival outweighs morals.

"I lucked upon a storm. One that beat me worse than any Tradey had before but a necessary element to my survival. The strong wind and current kept me up for three days straight. I had no feel for my heading and no time to consider it, really. I don't recall seeing the island, only waking on the beach on a bed of palm leaves. Before I could sit up, she was at my side with coconut juice and a wet cloth on my head."

"Samara..." Jeremiah whispers. He can see her through Demetrius's vision. She looks at Demetrius with the same dancing eyes from his dreams, silencing the same demons determined to break him.

"'Welcome to the land of the Living,' she said to me through a half smile. I remember because she had this way of saying things, like she was singing a song. Her eyes remind me of yours. They have a way of reading your soul's secrets and forgiving them at the same time. Well, if you have something needing forgiving anyways." Another cigar break. He reaches into the cherrywood box and hands another to Jeremiah who hadn't noticed that his own was burnt to the filter. With a scratchy throat and burning nose, he grabs the second cigar without hesitation. The act of smoking keeps him from fidgeting or eating the dessert Cookie had put out that neither of the men noticed. His stomach is already gurgling, not accustomed to such rich and abundant amounts of food.

"I stayed with Sam on the island. Her people, the Sprytes, had all been taken by the Command to Varthia. God only knows what they did to them. She was young and hid with an elder in the ocean when a ship came and took them. That elder had long passed when I arrived. Although Samara looked sixteen, she had been around for over eighty earth years. Sprytes age slowly."

Jeremiah interjects, "Samara. My mother was a Spryte?"

"Come on. You're a smart kid," Lord Demetrius eludes with condescending intention and continues.

"She and I grew fond of each other. I dare not say I know what love is, but our infatuation was close to it. Young and naive we figured we'd rule the world together. We spent many nights plotting our revenge on Varthia for my robbed childhood and her people getting taken. Then one day the ship came back but this time with Varthian officials. They were plotting out a second island for the Command to operate out of. Establishing a second Varthia, if you will, would give them an advantage to ruling the seas. I'll be damned if Sam didn't put up a fight for you and her."

Jeremiah's point of view changes. No longer is he looking at slides from Demetrius's perspective but as the infant in Samara's arms. She strokes his small cheek and rests him in a crib made of bamboo and palm trees. He sees the full moon staring down at him in beautiful serenity contradicting the bloody scene taking place.

Samara's scream pierces his ears as Lord Demetrius continues his narration. "I'd heard her painful cries and pleas for mercy, but by the time I arrived she'd been stabbed by Admiral Christoph Devonshire. I then took you to the Ascetics." Demetrius' cigar hits the filter. He puts it out on the cake Cookie had served them for dessert. He strikes a match and lights another cigar just as Jeremiah opens his eyes. "Well? Now you know. Does that provide insight into your past? Into why you were orphaned?"

"I told you I'm not looking for that. You volunteered the story." Jeremiah's defensive reaction says more to Lord Demetrius than intended.

"Let's try this instead. If you could ask me one question about my past, what would it be?" Lord Demetrius tests his character once more.

"How did you escape?" Jeremiah adds the ashes from his cigar onto the already ruined cake. The white frosting greys and drips from the droppings.

"Samara's people are ancient. They are good, but they are powerful. In order to sustain their power, they can transfer it to each other at the time of death, making each generation more powerful than the last. Even though I was a human and her people would have forbidden it, she passed it to me while she was dying. With Admiral Devonshire's sword still in her abdomen she reached out and passed her power to me, a human boy. Sprytes are good people, they don't use their powers to kill, only to heal and bring life. Being a human, I could harness the power to destroy. Being a man, I used the Spryte power to kill all but Victor who was my first transition. Lord Devonshire also escaped. I never found him."

He pauses once more, turning the cigar in his fingers. Jeremiah sits stunned by the tale of both of their births. The birth of a soon to be orphaned infant and the birth of a notorious vigilante. His view of the warmonger has shifted. There's no doubt that Lord Demetrius's vigilante mission is warranted, but does that make it right?

"Why are you telling me all of this?" Jeremiah huffs to his father.

Before Lord Demetrius can answer, Cookie enters the room and begins to blow out the candles and opens the windows to reveal a full moon for the fourth night in a row. Jeremiah can remember the number of full moons, but not his friends. He's forgotten them. Lord Demetrius's darkness clouds the front of his mind. Gone are the worries of drunk Tradeys, Bingley and Quinn's whereabouts or Demetrius's intentions with him. All he can focus on is Lord Demetrius and the key to his past. The key to his powers and what that key unlocks.

Victor enters the room again. "Begging your pardon once more, my Lord. I've adjusted our heading to Rosselyn. We will be arriving near sunrise." Jeremiah's studies on Knoen were vast, giving him knowledge of the island as soon as it's named. Rosselyn is very much governed by the Command. The last outpost East before you hit unchartered waters. Lost Soul Island is rumoured to lie in this direction, but no ship has been able to find it. Any that dare venture through the waters don't come back. Not alive, anyways. Taking away Rosselyn would give Lord Demetrius's mission an advantage over the Command, pushing their naval vessels back west to Varthia.

"Thank you, Victor, I'll meet you at the helm within the hour." Lord Demetrius shoos away his first mate with a stern, whole arm wave. "You'll come inland with us this time." Lord Demetrius instructs as he stands and grabs his coat. He walks to the exit and pauses momentarily. Jeremiah turns to watch him leave. Lord Demetrius stands on the edge of turning back to Jeremiah to say something but continues out the door and into the moonlit evening.

Chapter 25

Jeremiah expected another in-between with Samara, but it didn't come. Instead, he was one of Lord Demetrius's men. One of the transitioned, landing on the island of Varthia. Not on the sacred beach entrance to the Fringe, but instead on the Command's side of the island. A full-frontal attack on the black castle and Admiral Devonshire. The same Admiral that killed his mother.

"Lord Demetrius, the Liberator!" he shouted with hundreds of other men. They arrived on multiple ships speckling the reef like a plague of locusts with multiple Command vessels sinking in flames throughout. The Crystal Star shone red above, foreshadowing the futile bloodshed they were bringing. Once their ship was a mere hundred meters from the shore, they jumped out into waist deep water and rushed towards the island. A group of Varthian villagers wait on the shore for them, armed with pitchforks and swords. The castle itself features cannonball punctures and sounds of fighting from inside. The surrounding homes were engulfed in flames creating a backdrop of terror. Jeremiah looks to the transitioned men in uniformed formation walking steadily towards the shore, and spots Bingley leading the pack. His vivacious demeanor is replaced with a grimace that would make a grown man cry. Jeremiah never looked at him as intimidating before, but his raw expression of pure evil would instill terror in the bravest of men.

As the transitioned reach ankle deep water, the villagers make an ineffective attempt to stop them from entering the burning town of Varthia. Transitioned Bingley waves a giant metal star over his head and makes two big swings to take out ten villagers, a knife through warm butter. Jeremiah locks eyes with one untouched villager who instantly recognizes him. Keedo, the boy from the Tradey slave ship that sunk just outside Varthia, shipwrecking Jeremiah to the Fringe. He marches towards Jeremiah with purpose in his eyes and a sword in his hand. Keedo slices the head off one of the transitioned with his eyes still locked on target. He starts to run at Jeremiah who looks to his right hand and sees his sword glistening with the red of the Crystal Star. Jeremiah gets into a fighting stance and charges towards Keedo. Their swords meet with a clang of metal. Jeremiah disarms Keedo within seconds and holds his sword to the boy's throat.

"You have been destined for this evil since the day I met you. It's your fault they are all dead." Keedo spits disdain and points towards the island. Jeremiah looks to where Keedo is pointing to see a charred willow tree with bodies hanging from the burning limbs. Sydney's blue, lifeless body looks the same as when Jeremiah last saw it drowned underwater in that Tradey slave transport. She holds hands with her younger sister Scotty who is missing both of her eyes. Those big eyes that were once so full of life. Above her is Anuva with writing quills sticking all over him like a pincushion. The final body belongs to Quinn. Naked and cut open, she hangs with eyes wide open and an expression of horror that buckles Jeremiah's knees. He maintains a sword over Keedo's throat, slightly piercing through his skin from the mere sharpness of the blade.

"This has always been your fate. Blood for blood, Lord Jeremiah." Keedo presses his neck closer to the blade, making it pierce his neck even more.

"Your weakness is offensive," Gregor's words come out of Jeremiah's mouth as involuntary as breathing. He slices Keedo's throat, spilling his blood into the ocean water.

Varthia's Crystal Star flag has been replaced with a simple black one, signaling the victorious capture of Varthia and doom of the Command.

"Lord Jeremiah, the Liberator!" Bingley shouts in a booming voice that echoes throughout Varthia's city. Jeremiah looks up to Quinn's lifeless body hanging in the tree and sees her lips moving.

"Save us, Jer," she whispers to him in a barely audible volume.

"Wake up and save us!" Her voice rings through his ears and wakes him from the in-between. He breathes heavy, coughing hard into his hands. Blackness appears that he assumes is from the cigars he had mere hours ago. Dawn is close, but he won't sleep again. Instead, he stands up and reaches for his clothes. He is aware of the heaviness on his chest once more. Aware of what he needs to do now that he remembers her. He remembers Quinn.

Chapter 26

Jeremiah races out of his room mid-way through sliding a white shirt over his head. He remembers Quinn. His stomach twists with the guilt of forgetting her and anger with Lord Demetrius. Angry, yet conflicted. There's no denying his relationship with his father influences the anger he feels for Lord Demetrius. He races towards the stairs to the helm where Lord Demetrius sleeps. The sky above turns pink through grey skies. A warning of rough waters ahead.

Lord Demetrius sits on a chair on the helm with his boots crossed and his captain's hat covering his face. Jeremiah can hear him sleeping, deep breath in and slow breath out, but wheezing through his tired lungs. He raises the sword above his head and brings it down to Lord Demetrius's neck and stops it before hitting him. 'Dammit, Jer, just do it!' he thinks to himself. This man would kill you in a heartbeat. But would he? He raises the sword over his head again and counts down '1, 2, 3 and go!' he thinks, but stops just at the Lord's neck once more. It's not that simple.

"Rise and shine, Lord Demetrius." Jeremiah wakes his father with the point of Crippen's sword on his throat.

"Jeremiah, I was wondering when you'd wake." Lord Demetrius smiles at his son but does not stand.

"Wake from the darkness you had clouding my mind?" he challenges him.

"A darkness you welcomed, if I remember correctly. Jeremiah, what is it you want?" Lord Demetrius slides his Varthian captain's hat onto his slicked back hair.

"Let Quinn and Bingley go, or I swear I'll spill your blood right here and right now." A threat he wasn't sure he could keep. Lord Demetrius slides his tongue inside his teeth making a 'tsk tsk' sound.

"You already tried twice, my son. It was never my intention to harm or hold the girl hostage. You may both leave on the next island, but I'm afraid the giant cannot leave me. He's transitioned, you see. He needs my power to live." Lord Demetrius strikes a cigar slowly so as not to frighten Jeremiah into cutting him open. The boy stands for a moment, surveying his options.

"What island is our heading?" he asks, keeping the tip of his blade on Lord Demetrius's throat.

"We'll land on Othex. It's a deserted trading island that the Command shutdown a decade ago. I'll leave you provisions should you wish it, although I would hope you'd join me willingly on my mission to Varthia. Surely both you and the girl have interests in taking the Command," Lord Demetrius suggests.

"Why don't you stay with us? Leave this mission and come live with us!" A suggestion Jeremiah didn't think he'd ever make, but as soon as the idea slipped out of his mouth, it felt right. "Vengeance won't bring my mother back. It won't resurrect Samara. She's dead, but we are here." Now he is pleading with his father and not threatening the great Lord Demetrius. His sword drops to the ground.

"It's not about me, Jeremiah. I wish you could see that. My motives have never been so selfish. Our world needs to be free of the Command's thumb of tyranny." Lord Demetrius throws his cigar in the ocean and stands. He isn't much taller than Jeremiah. In fact, without his boots they may be the same height. He reaches a hand on his son's shoulder and looks into his blue eyes.

"Jeremiah, I'll take you to Quinn." He smiles at his son who smiles back. A spark ignites and the darkness in Lord Demetrius's black eyes start to lighten.

"Lord Demetrius, Quinn still insists on complete segregation. I'm afraid the men didn't know her upon capture, and she remains frightened," Victor speaks from the deck, breaking the moment between Lord Demetrius and Jeremiah.

"Show her to me," Jeremiah demands.

"I'm not sure it wise. We tried to calm her with the giant, but she cut her arms, screaming that it was a trick by Lord Demetrius. Might be best to wait until we land. Should be in Othex by dusk." Victor scribbles in his notebook while speaking. Jeremiah's stomach drops at the thought of Quinn hurting herself. She must be so scared. He looks to Lord Demetrius who has turned to face the seas.

"Victor, would you escort Jeremiah for the day? I'll tend to Quinn," Lord Demetrius instructs. Jeremiah doesn't like this plan. He wants to see Quinn himself and know she is alive. As though Lord Demetrius could hear his thoughts, he speaks into his mind with his back still facing the ocean. 'I'll put her into a deep sleep with visions of Spryte people on the Fringe and only wake her upon our arrival. You have no reason not to trust me, Jeremiah.' Lord Demetrius walks past his son and disappears below deck, leaving Jeremiah in Victor's care for the last time.

Chapter 27

"How much do you know about Sprytes?" Victor asks Jeremiah while motioning with his head for the boy to follow him. With his book in his hands, the distinguished man strolls towards the escape boats where Jeremiah first saw Lord Demetrius.

"Not much. My mother was one and my father has some of their powers harnessed. Quinn tells me they manipulate the forest in Varthia to protect the Fringe people." Jeremiah's heart twinges saying her name. The thought of her suffering alone and frightened is more than he can bear.

Victor nods his head. "You have some of that power too, you know. Being half Spryte and half human is a rarity. Never in all my lifetime have I come across a half-breed. At least, not that I can recollect. Lord Demetrius's power seems to fade memories the longer you are under his incantation, but your knowledge always remains. Ask me anything. Would you like to know more?"

Jeremiah's heart skips a beat. In all his readings at Knoen, he never came across Spryte colonies. Likely, the Command hid anything in order to alter their history. Knowing that Victor was of The Command and yet has knowledge of the Spryte people makes his background curiouser and curiouser. He nods to Victor, hardly containing his excitement.

"There is legend and there are myths. Legend tells of their beginnings. Tipray, deity of water, who caused the great flood had a sister Lillius, deity of land, who loved humans. She selected few good souls and breathed into them a portion of her power. The gods and deities are a little much for my liking, but people must have an explanation for everything, mustn't they? Lillius didn't realize the extent of her action. With her power, all evil and destructive human tendencies disappeared from the Sprytes. What remained were pure souls who used their powers for good and never for bad. They healed, they gave life and they made their mortal brothers and sisters better people. In essence, they were ironically better people than we humans could possibly be. Seeing these perfect beings made Tipray angry. He hated what his sister had done as humanity was perfectly destructive and evil in his eyes. He locked his sister in a dungeon in the deepest depth of the ocean and raised the waters to flood and cause destruction back into the world." Victor grabbed an apple from his pocket and took a large bite of it.

"The Lillius story on Knoen is similar, but it doesn't contain anything of the Spryte legend." Jeremiah leans on the side of the ship, questioning everything he learned on Knoen.

"Aye, I'm sure it does. The Command is more oppressive than you could possibly imagine. Stripping knowledge from its knowledgeable creates a controlled environment. It's all from fear, Jeremiah. They fear the Sprytes and anything they don't fully understand. There was a Command scientist who wanted to experiment on them, believing they were simply evolved humans, but they are a stealthy creature changing forms in the blink of an eye. They mostly take a vegetation form, but once, I swear, I witnessed a small child turn into a mouse and scurry down a hole. One of the memories still kicking around in this head of mine." Victor taps on his head with a juicy apple in hand before throwing it into the sea. "Your father, our Lord, is the only human I know who has Lillius' power running through him."

"He isn't a Spryte, though. He is a human and humans are the most vile and evil race in the world, right?" Jeremiah continues. "Wouldn't that mean he can't use the powers for good? Only bad?" Jeremiah questions.

"I'm afraid it's not that simple, my boy. This is new territory for Spryte powers. One thing is for certain, unlike the Spryte people, he has the capability to use the powers in a bad form. Instead of being limited to giving life and healing, he can take life and he can destroy." Victor continues along the side of the ship, tucking a loose hair behind his ear.

"Victor, you believe in what my father... what Lord Demetrius is doing is right?" Jeremiah asks. His mind in a quarrel.

"My boy, I believe he is doing something and isn't that enough? I can't pretend to know right from wrong, but I do believe in him. He needs more men, but I believe in his plan. I believe by the end of this mission, the Command will be finished and Varthia's age of tyranny will be completed. That's a vision I would unite behind repeatedly. Lord Demetrius the Liberator!" Victor calls and is met with men across the ship returning the cry: "Lord Demetrius the Liberator!"

"You didn't choose this, though. His powers are making you believe it. They are making you obey, aren't they?"

Victor grasps his chest, feeling the same heaviness Jeremiah feels. His grey features shimmer in the rising sun.

"Lord Demetrius's powers are strong, and they force your free will, but I still have a mind of my own, boy. I would join him without protest again and again if he asked, but I must say that his power helps. It connects us. He communicates with us without speaking and can transition us from creature to human form in a matter of seconds."

"You mean those creatures in the Fringe were Lord Demetrius's men?" Jeremiah stops and remembers the creature who Cornelius killed. He remembers its smell and the gaze it held on him like a wolf on the brink of a kill.

Victor stops Jeremiah and places his hand on his shoulder.

"They were and are. Jeremiah, you have this Spryte power too. The Lord could teach you. He's been searching for you for a long time, you know. Looking for his son, the half Spryte. One that may even be more powerful than Lord Demetrius himself."

Crippen appears behind Victor with a bandana, wiping sweat off his wrinkly forehead. "Victor, might I borrow the lad a moment. I could use a strong arm to tighten the ropes on the sails, ya see. The others are getting gear together for Othex.." His raspy voice sounds as though he'd been smoking for years.

"Yes, just bring him back. We should be reaching the island in a couple of hours." Victor places his hand on Jeremiah's back and slides him forward to go with Crippen.

Chapter 28

"Land Ho!" Crippen's voice bellows with a crackle and squeak across the deck of *Hades Pride*. Jeremiah had moved on from tightening the sails to mopping the deck. His hair has grown to the nape of his neck now, slightly curled inward from the salty sea air. He drops the mop onto the old wooden deck and hits the bucket of water over, rushing to get a glimpse of the island that will be his new home. His oasis with Quinn. He pushes long locks of black hair out of his face and gazes into the distance, squinting to get a better glimpse. A whistle comes from above and Crippen yells, "Tis your island of destiny, young Jeremiah! Your new home awaits!" and laughs in a full belly way that would have been warming if it came from Bingley, but gives a menacing tone coming from him. Jeremiah pays no attention, everything in his body wants to jump off this ship and swim ashore with Quinn. To start a new life away from vendettas of grown men. He longs for Bingley to join them, but with Lord Demetrius's curse on him, he can't.

"You'll be happy here?" Lord Demetrius appears behind Jeremiah. "All I want is for you to be happy, my son. I wish it was with me, but I understand."

"You could stay with us, you know," Jeremiah pleads once more.

"I'll accompany you to shore. It's the least and yet the most I can do." Lord Demetrius puts a hand on Jeremiah's shoulder and the boy seizes the opportunity to hug his father.

"The escape boat is ready for you to board," Victor interrupts to point further down the ship's hull. Jeremiah sees Quinn sitting in the ship with her back to them. Her blonde hair tousled together in dreadlocks. They climb in and Quinn's face lights up at the sight of Jeremiah. She leaps into his arms, knocking him off-balance and almost taking the escape boat off the pulley system.

"I've been so lost," she whispers to him.

"I've found you," he whispers back. "How did you come out of your trance?" he asks, and she answers by simply looking at Lord Demetrius. He tilts his captain's hat towards them.

"It was not easy. I specialize in inflicting the damage and not so much reversing it, but you have a strong woman here."

They reach the water and Jeremiah grabs the oars to guide them onto the shore. The island itself is small, but lush. Golden sand sparkles in the sun along the shore, a beacon showing them the way in. There is a long pier stretching from the shore, broken in more than one place. Damaged from the strong sea storms no doubt. They sit in silence on the escape boat. Quinn, at the edge of her seat, looking towards the beach.

Looking towards their new home, Jeremiah finds himself looking at Demetrius who himself stares blankly ahead at the island. His eyes look more blue as they stray further away from *Hades Pride*. In them he sees more sadness than ever before. A man who spent years looking for his son only for him to be gone in the blink of an eye. Only for him to choose not to follow in an expected path. To follow and join a father's mission. They reach the shore to find rundown buildings, weathered and unkempt. Lord Demetrius coughs more blood into a white cloth before getting out of the ship and hugging his son into him.

"Goodbye, Demetrius," Jeremiah says and releases his hold on his father who could almost pass for a real man now and not the tyrant of the sea.

"Whatever happens, know that I love you." Lord Demetrius releases his grip on his son. Jeremiah looks to his father in confusion; wanting to ask what could possibly happen.

"Hello, hero," a voice Jeremiah knows all too well sings from behind them. Charlotte appears out of one of the battered buildings along with a dozen Varthian uniformed soldiers. Quinn tries to run, but one of the men stops her. She connects the officer with a right hook and grabs his sword from the holster in one swift motion but is muscled into constraint. Jeremiah rushes towards them but stops when another man shouts from behind him.

"One more step and your father dies." He turns to see a decorated Varthian Officer holding a dagger to Lord Demetrius's throat.

"Thank you for the return of my daughter, Lord Demetrius. I suppose it's only fair. I gave you your son and you return my daughter." Charlotte rubs her bone-like pale finger across Quinn's face all the while smiling at Jeremiah. Another man enters from behind a wall of palm trees. His uniform shows him to not just be an officer of the Command, but Admiral Devonshire himself.

"Commander Shwark, blindfold Lord Demetrius and bind him," The Admiral instructs the man holding Lord Demetrius who instantly wraps a cloth over his eyes.

Jeremiah straddles the ground between Quinn and his father, waiting for their fate. The Admiral stands taller than any of the other men. Jet black hair covers most of his head except for two grey streaks that run just above his ears. He walks towards Lord Demetrius with a distinguished and arrogant manner. Commander Shwark kicks Demetrius behind his knees, making him kneel before the Leader of the Command. Devonshire bends at the waist to whisper into Lord Demetrius's ear.

"Make one move and I will have both of them killed. Make no mistake, I may be a man of the law, but I have ways of making people disappear," he threatens Lord Demetrius who remains silent and willing.

"Take these Varthian dressings off him. Tattered and old as they may be, they are still too worthy of this trash." Schwark slides his sword down Lord Demetrius's back and cuts the uniform off him. Demetrius's naked body is covered with scars all over, signifying the battles he had fought. Signifying no matter how powerful, he is still human.

"Demetrius, do something!" Jeremiah shouts causing Charlotte to laugh uncontrollably, reminding him of Trish.

"Had he taught you nothing upon that ship? Stupid hero. He can't use his powers if it means your life would be threatened. It's why your mother, that filthy Spryte whore, gave them to him to begin with. It's why he left you on Knoen. You are a hindrance to the great Lord Demetrius." Charlotte walks towards Lord Demetrius, taking a sword from one of the Varthian soldiers along the way.

"Allow me to demonstrate," she sneers and slices Lord Demetrius across the chest. Not deep enough to kill, but enough to make him scream in pain.

"Ah, the great Lord Demetrius really can bleed." She smiles; a woman exceptionally pleased with herself.

Admiral Devonshire stands behind Lord Demetrius and addresses the Varthian soldiers, Charlotte, Quinn and Jeremiah.

"To my fellow comrades and prisoners: Today will go down in history as the day we put an end to the tyranny, destruction and life of Lord Demetrius. The

213

number one threat to the Command and Varthia. Too long has our battle of strength and wit been tested and tried by this evil man. Too many women and children lived in fear of the great Lord Demetrius. For too long have we wasted the Command's resources on hunting this man instead of finishing Varthia's missions." Devonshire takes his sword out of its holster. The blade sparkles with the sunlight.

"By the power invested in me by the Varthian Command and to those who pay witness, I, Admiral Devonshire, sentence Lord Demetrius, Captain of *Hades Pride*, conqueror of the sea and king of Lost Soul Island to death." He lifts his sword into the sky and brings it down upon Lord Demetrius's neck, separating his head from his body. The lifeless head of Lord Demetrius rolls along the sand and his body slides to the ground.

Jeremiah cries out to the sky as the heaviness that was once on his chest releases with the death of Lord Demetrius. The death of his father. Quinn screams out from behind him, still constrained by an officer. Admiral Devonshire takes Lord Demetrius's sword and places it beside Jeremiah.

"I am a man of honour and code. This is for you to fight for your life upon this lonely island. Even if you do kill the dozen officers I leave here, you'll be marooned on this desolate island for the rest of your life." Admiral Devonshire snaps his fingers, commanding a few of the officers and Shwark to disappear into the vegetation of the island. Charlotte grabs Quinn by the wrist to drag her with them.

"I won't go anywhere with you!" Quinn spits in her mother's face.

"Children can be so disappointing, but I know how to break you." Charlotte nods to an officer of the Command who hits Quinn, sending her unconscious. Jeremiah doesn't notice. He is kneeling on the ground, staring at his father's headless body. He holds the sword in his hands and closes his eyes. A hate fills inside of him. A hate for taking him away from Anuva. A hate for being sold to Gregor on Jopwen. A hate for Charlotte taking Quinn away. A hate for the death of his father. A hate for the Command. A hate that takes the form of a black liquid, filling his veins. The Spryte power in a human form, dangerous and evil. The Varthian officers left to kill Jeremiah approach him cautiously, hearing his deep breaths in and out. The blue skies turn black with thunderous clouds above the island of Othex. His eyes are closed, but he can feel them edging closer to him. He can smell their fear and sense their presence. A sensory system clicks into place. Opening his eyes to view his surrounding, their once blue colour changes to blackness.

He grips his father's sword in his hands, ready to avenge him. With a smirk on his face and a newfound connection to his Spryte power he asks the officers, "Are you ready?"

Chapter 29

Aboard *Hades Pride*, Victor paces. He squints towards the island that is covered in vegetation, impatient for what will come. He holds onto the side of *Hades Pride*, pushing splinters into his forefingers, anxious for movement in the distance. Lord Demetrius had confided in him only a week prior on his plans, along the coast of the Varthian Fringe when they were preparing to invade and find Lord Demetrius's son.

*****

"The boy is the answer," Lord Demetrius told Victor as he coughs blood into a handkerchief. He holds it close and winces with the last cough of red. Sitting on his bed in the captain's chambers. This is the only place he can have privacy to confide in Victor.

"He is the only one who can finish what we started and what I cannot see to the end." Lord Demetrius is weakened. The strain of the Spryte power is too much for his human body. Whether it's the length of time he's allowed the darkness to flow through him or the strength it took to control the army he has created, Lord Demetrius was dying.

"What if he doesn't? What if he decides not to? My Lord, he barely knows you. You must not leave your work unfinished," Victor pleads with him.

"He'll do it, Victor. With a push in the right direction, he'll see the only way to beat the Varthian Command is by using his powers for destruction. He is the only one who can retake this world, so we can truly be free. His mother died for this." Lord Demetrius pulls himself up from the bed and straightens his posture, attempting to hide the sickness taking him.

"You won't feel me leave you as the darkness won't lift. My death is futile, but I can transfer my power to him and, combined with his own, he'll be the enemy needed to destroy Varthia. Trust me, Victor, and help Jeremiah stay steady on course." Lord Demetrius dusts off his comrade's shoulder and looks him in the eye before walking out the door of his cabin into the glowing night and is welcomed by his men.

"But he's just a boy," Victor whispers.

*****

A thud on the deck boards makes Victor's heart jump into his throat. He turns around to see a lit cigar billowing smoke from underneath Lord Demetrius's captain's hat.

"Sir, what happened to Jeremiah?" Victor asks while anxiously rubbing his hands.

217

The figure steps out of the shadows to expose a younger version of Lord Demetrius. Jeremiah lifts the brim of his father's hat, revealing his eyes to Victor. Black and complete with the dark.

"Sail ahead," Jeremiah commands.

"Where is our heading?" Victor asks like second nature, looking to his new captain for a course.

Jeremiah takes a long haul of the cigar.

"We're going to Varthia to finish this." He exhales a dark cloud of smoke that drifts towards a crescent moon.